MYSTERIOUS TALES

from

TURTON TOWER

Peter S Farley BA (Hons)

Published by: www.grandpatravels.com

Yo Richard keep looking for orbs!

Peter S. Farley.

17.10.2018

ACKNOWLEDGEMENTS

The writer wishes to thank all contributors and especially Mr John Gardiner and Doreen Hough for providing information which made it possible to write this account.

Thanks are also extended to the staff of Bolton Library Archives Department. Their help in allowing the writer to see newspapers, photographs and documents that are relevant to this subject is greatly appreciated.

DEDICATION

This work is dedicated to the people of Turton and environs and to all students of the paranormal.

ABOUT THE AUTHOR

The author has been intrigued by the subject of the paranormal for many years. He has personal experience of inexplicable happenings and believes what he knows to be true. Although at the same time he keeps an open mind on the subject. The writer would like to point out that he does not have definite answers to the many questions raised by the mysterious tales from Turton Tower. For the most part he can only offer more questions.

"I have no answers; I can only offer more questions"
Peter S Farley

Table of Contents

INTRODUCTION

Close to the Lancashire village of Chapeltown, stands Turton Tower, which has been described as one of the 'most interesting structures in the neighbourhood of Bolton.' [1] There can be little doubt that the statement is based upon truth. Historical records are uncertain about when and by whom the Tower was first built but it is generally accepted that it was constructed sometime during the 1400's. Once a site had been carefully chosen, it was constructed in the peel fashion. The finished edifice looked like a giant rectangular chimney but at that time, the stone built structure was the most economical and practical form of defence against would-be predators. If danger presented itself, the owner, together with his people and any livestock, could gather together inside the Tower and there they might feel relatively safe.

As the passing decades morphed into centuries, certain successive owners of the Tower, added to it their preferred style of architecture. There is a section that is Elizabethan whilst another is of the Victorian era and collectively they culminate to present a visual feast. As one might expect with a building of such advanced years, its existence has spawned a number of mysterious tales. The tales relate to supernatural happenings both at and within the vicinity of the Tower. This literary work is designed to bond the tales together into a single narrative.

Three distinctly different buildings and each sited at separate locations, are mentioned throughout the text. They are Timberbottom Farm, Bradshaw Hall and Turton Tower. All of which seem to be inextricably linked, either by accident or design. Was it merely a coincidence that Turton Tower was beginning to function as a museum, at the time when Bradshaw Hall and Timberbottom Farm were in the throes of being demolished? Similarly, was it also a coincidence that the writer should be available when the various 'mysterious tales' were poised to be recorded, or perhaps 'lost' forever?

It was Carl Yung, a Swiss psychologist, who in the 1920s described the word synchronicity as being the experience of two or more separate and dissimilar events which are then found to be meaningfully related, where they are unlikely to be casually related. The two events cannot be attributed to the cause and effect theory but are rather a simultaneous blending together in an inexplicable yet highly meaningful way. [2] Synchronicity seems to be far more than just coincidence. To express this idea in another and hopefully more understandable way, the following anecdote is used.

The French writer Emile Deschamps describes in his memoirs a time during the year of 1805 when he was given some plum pudding, by a man named Monsieur de Fontgibu, whom he describes as a 'stranger.' Ten years later whilst sitting in a Parisian restaurant, that bore no connection to his earlier experience, he saw that plum pudding was listed on the menu. When he came to order a portion, the waiter informed him that the last of the pudding had already been served to another gentleman. It transpired that the 'other gentleman' was none other than Monsieur de Fontgibu!

Again, many years later, in 1832, Emile Deschamps was enjoying a meal with some friends and when the time arrived, he ordered what by now must have been one of his favourite desserts. It was of course; plum pudding. He thoughtfully recalled his earlier experiences revolving around plum pudding and whimsically announced that all that was needed, to complete his dinner, was the presence of Monsieur de Fontgibu. No sooner had he uttered the sentence when who should shuffle into the room, albeit showing signs of age but Monsieur Fontgibu himself! [3]

I, the writer, felt somewhat like Emile when my first visit to Turton Tower kick-started a chain of events. On numerous occasions I had unwittingly passed by Turton Tower whilst travelling by railway carriage or by automobile. This was because of the fact that the Tower is set back from the main road and is not easily noticeable to passersby.

Ultimately, I paid my first visit to the Tower in the year 2011. A guide showed me around the labyrinth of passages and rooms. He explained about the history of the buildings and the people who had lived there. I was overawed by the magnitude of the interior and the quantity of artefacts that were displayed. Being somewhat receptive to things of a paranormal nature, I wasn't surprised to 'feel' a 'presence,' as we crossed the main wooden staircase and enter the Drawing Room. Of course, at that time I had no knowledge of any ghostly happenings that may have been recorded at the Tower. But that state of play was to change in subsequent months.

I later joined a group of volunteers known as the 'Friends of Turton Tower.' They organise functions to help raise funds. Their efforts contribute to ensure that the Tower remains open and its contents are available for the public to enjoy. Because of my involvement with them, I have been able to gather many stories that relate to the 'happenings,' both in and around the Tower. In light of all of this, I am persuaded to wonder if my involvement is not another example of synchronicity.

I was conscious of the notion that when a story is repeated throughout the years, there is a tendency for its detail to change. I therefore made every possible effort to get close to the original source. Whenever I saw newspaper reports where names of people were mentioned, I made a point to see if the person in question was still alive and if so to speak to them personally. In short I have endeavoured to present a collection of accounts and relevant information that is as accurate as can be.

At numerous places throughout the text I have used the heading 'Writer's Note.' After which I have added some comments regarding the mysterious activities that are being described. However, on no pretext do I profess to have the answers; indeed all I can provide are more questions! In the end it is you, the reader, who must look at the evidence put before you and decide. Do you believe that paranormal activities occur at Turton Tower, or do they not?

CHRONOLOGY OF EVENTS

[1542 - 1949] Bradshaw Hall

[1683 - 1959] Timberbottom Farm

[1848 - 1963] Bradshaw Bleach-Works

[1871- 1948] Col. H. M. Hardcastle (Bradshaw Hall)

[1857-1928] Sir Lees-Knowles (Turton Tower)

[1930] On October 14 1930 Lady Nina Knowles (wife of Sir Lees Knowles) presented Turton Tower and its grounds to Turton Urban District Council.

[1934] On August 9th 1934 Lady Nina Knowles formally handed over the Tower to the Council of Turton.

[1932 - 1948] Mark Ashworth (Custodian of Turton Tower) (None Resident) N.B. Not related to Ald. George H. Ashworth.

[1865-1954] Alderman, George Harry Ashworth

[1952] Turton Tower was officially opened as a Museum on 25 June 1952 by the Rt. Hon., the Earl of Derby, M.C., J.P., Lord Lieutenant of Lancashire.

[1948-1965] Doreen Hough (nee Pike) & Family (Custodians of Turton Tower) - (Resident)

[1965-1968] The Weatherall Family (Custodians of Turton Tower) - (Resident)

[1972-1975] The Walker Family (Custodians of Turton Tower) - (Resident)

[1989] Demolition of Bradshaw Bleach Works chimney

[2008 - 2014] John Gardiner (Custodian of Turton Tower) - (None Resident)

GLOSSARY

The following glossary of terms is included to enable the reader to have a clearer understanding of the events being described.

BOGGART

A 'boggart' is one of numerous terms used in English folklore to denote a household spirit that causes mischief and things to disappear, milk to sour, or dogs to go lame.

SPIRIT

The writer Nandor Fodor describes spirit as 'the divine particle, the vital essence, and the inherent actuating element in life' [4] He says that 'spirit' dwells in the astral body or the soul. It may also be noted that in many religious philosophies the terms 'spirit and 'soul' are used interchangeably. Thomas Grimshaw said, "Spirits are real people, human beings; men, women and children stripped of their outer garment of flesh, but still possessed of a real, substantial body that we know as the spiritual body." [5] Andrew Jackson Davis said, "The term 'spirit' is used to signify the centre most principle of man's existence, the divine energy or life of the soul of Nature.

In yet other language, 'soul' is the life of the outer body and the 'spirit' is the life of the soul. After physical death, the 'soul' or life of the material body becomes the form or body of the eternal spirit" [6] 'Spirit' can be described as the innermost core of a deceased personality. It is the term used for the intelligence contacted by a medium at a séance. A 'spirit' can, therefore, manifest in various forms. It can actually appear through materializations, making use of a medium's ectoplasm, and it can make its presence felt through such tools as automatic writing, psychokinesis, apports, and the like.

SPIRIT WORLD

Thomas Grimshaw would have us believe that the 'Spirit World' is a real world, which is just as real to spirits who function through their spiritual bodies, as the physical world is to us, who function through our physical bodies. He adds that it is the place where we make our homes after transitioning from the earth plane. He maintains that the spirit world is the level of existence where there are no boundaries, as we know them on earth; no boundaries of time, space, and tangibility. Besides this there are no divisions, as in the Christian concept of 'Heaven' and 'Hell' and no 'purgatory' as understood by the Roman Catholics. The spirit world is just one place; neither 'good' nor 'bad' and having neither rewards nor punishments. [7]

Maurice Barbanell maintains that what is called the 'Spirit World,' is not some far-off geographically situated planet, but rather a part of the universe in which we live. He believes there are no hard and fast boundaries between this world and what is wrongly called the next but that they are both parts of one universe, and these aspects mingle and blend and merge all the time. Because of the constant, growing materialism in which man lives, he more or less automatically cuts himself off from the spiritual world, which is as much a part of his natural habitat as is the physical world. This is one of the reasons why so many primitive people remain naturally psychic because they live close to nature. They haven't become town dwellers forced into materialistic pursuits in order to make a living, so they are normally accessible to the more subtle vibrations of the spirit world. [8]

POLTERGEIST

The literal meaning of the word poltergeist is 'noisy ghost,' which is derived from the German words 'polte' meaning 'noise' and 'geist' meaning 'spirit'. It seems not to be a spirit in the sense of being the ethereal body of one who is deceased, but seems instead to be a discarnate entity or raw energy field. Poltergeist activity often takes place around an adolescent going through puberty, or someone in a highly emotional state. The person is usually unaware of the pent-up energy being randomly released in his or her vicinity until the poltergeist activity explodes.

Objects will defy gravity and fly through the air, be moved around tables and other surfaces, lights will turn on and off, doors will open and close of their own volition, glass and china will be levitated and then smashed.

TELEKINESIS
Telekinesis is the movement of objects by spirits. An example would be the falling of a picture off a wall at the moment of someone's death.

APPORTATION
Apportation is similar to telekinesis, although the object is usually moved from one dimension to another. There is a commonality between telekinesis and the movement of objects attributed to poltergeists. When objects are moved by spirit the object usually moves smoothly. Poltergeist energy is such that the object moves unpredictably and erratically.

CLAIRALIENCE or CLAIRGUSTANCE
Clairalience or clairgustance means 'clear smelling'. At times when a spirit is or has been present, a smell of flowers, or perfume, or a particular tobacco can be present in the air.

GHOST or APPARITION
Ghost or apparition are words that are used to refer to the same thing. A ghost is an apparition or vision of a spirit of the dead. Ghosts can be of deceased people, animals or even of inanimate objects such as automobiles or trains. A ghost is generally thought of as a vague shadowy figure or a transparent figure in white, whilst an apparition tends to appear solid like a normal living being.

PARANORMAL
The term paranormal relates to happenings which are observed by one or more persons but that which do not fit into the present scientific paradigm.

TIMBERBOTTOM FARM

Photo No 1 (circa: 1959)
A view of Timberbottom farm buildings

This narrative has its beginning at a place called Bradshaw, which is a suburb of the Lancashire town of Bolton. Take a drive from Bolton's town centre along Tonge Moor Road and head in the direction of Bradshaw. As the road changes its name to Bradshaw Brow, look to the right and before reaching the junction of the A6059 and the A676, there is a street that is simply named, 'Timberbottom'.

At the end of the street is a cluster of modern houses that are built on the site of a demolished farm property. The centuries old farm was called 'Timberbottom.' Its name would probably have faded into obscurity, had it not been for the day when the remains of two human skulls were discovered.
A book titled 'Lancashire Legends' (1873) gives a brief outline of the history of the skulls.

> 'At a short distance from the Tower [Turton Tower] there is a farmhouse, known by the name of Timberbottom, or the Skull House. It is so called from the circumstance that two skulls are or were kept here, one of which was much decayed, and the other appeared to have been cut through by a blow from some sharp instrument. Tradition says that these skulls must be kept in the house, or the inmates will

12

never cease to be disturbed. They are said to have been buried many times in the graveyard at Bradshaw Chapel but they have always had to be exhumed and brought back to the farmhouse. They have even been thrown into the adjacent river, but to no purpose; for they had to be fished up and restored to their old quarters before the ghosts of their owners could once more rest in peace.' [9]

Six years later, J. D. Greenhalgh's book titled 'Notes on the History of the Township of Breightmet' (1879), records an account that was told to him by an elderly lady. She claimed to be related to the Smith family who had lived at Timberbottom Farm during the 17th century and could remember a story that was passed down the family from each generation.

One fateful night, so the story goes, the Smith family left the farmhouse in the care of a man-servant and went on their way. Now whether their departure was pre-planned and the word had got about, or whether it was just by chance is not mentioned but later that same evening the man-servant heard the approach of horses. At first he may have thought that the tenants of the farm were returning from their outing but very soon he became aware that the visitors were strangers and possibly would-be robbers.

He kept himself out of sight until he realised what they intended to do. This became apparent, when one of the robbers attempted to gain entry to the house, by means of an 'upper room' window. The man-servant rushed to the room, which was normally used to store cheese and on his way there made as much noise as he could. He was hoping to give the impression that he was not alone in the house. By the time he had reached the 'old cheese-room' he saw that the robber had already pushed his head through the open window and was about to climb into the room.

Wasting no time, the man-servant grabbed a 'huge cheese-knife' which he saw nearby and with a swipe or two cleaved off the robber's head! The head dropped to the floor and the robber's headless body slumped backwards, falling to the yard outside.

A second robber made a determined attempt to gain entry to the room but he too met with a disastrous end. His severed head joined company with that of his comrade and his headless body also fell to the ground. The bloody sight must have struck fear into the hearts of the remaining robbers. Their fear was such that they were compelled to hastily sling the blooded corpses across their horses' back and gallop away.

It is said that that they raced towards the village of Turton and in their wake left a trail of blood on the road. [10] Oh my, what a shocking home coming that must have been for the Smith family! What followed later is not recorded but presumably if the story is true, then the heads must have been kept at the farmhouse until their flesh had decayed and they had ultimately transformed into skulls.

Photo No 2 (circa: 1950s)
View of Timberbottom farm buildings

J. D. Greenhalgh's book includes an additional account regarding the history of the skulls, as related to him by a lady who was then turned seventy years of age. She remembered that a young servant lad by the name of Davenport, had been raised by the Smith family and lived at the farm. From her account it would seem that the skulls were kept permanently in the 'old cheese-room'. One day, Davenport, for whatever reason is not stated, declaring that the skulls should no longer remain in the house, took it upon himself to remove them from their resting place and throw them into the nearby Bradshaw Brook, at a spot known as 'Labby's Hole.'

Strange as it seemed, very soon after he had completed his task, such 'disturbances' began at the farm that resulted in no one being able to sleep too well. It didn't take long for the farm people to associate the nocturnal disturbances with the moving of the skulls. Therefore it was decided that they should be 'fished up' out of the brook and returned to their original place of rest at the farm. Although the task was described as a 'troublesome job,' they were ultimately retrieved and put back into the old cheese room. [11]

The lady's account further revealed that some twenty years prior to her statement, which would be about the year 1859, the skulls were removed again from the 'old cheese room' and taken to Bradshaw Hall. The Hall was the home of Thomas Hardcastle, J.P. and his sons, who were the owners of Timberbottom Farm and the attendant lands. One can only speculate as to what dialogue must have transpired when the skulls changed hands, so to speak. Presumably the tenants would have had to explain to their landlord as to how they had come by the skulls; but had they told the truth; or had they fabricated a convincing story?

Perhaps worth considering is one of the tales that have filtered down through the years. It allows people to believe that the skulls were originally dug up on the river bank, that was near to the farm. This would be a reasonable story to accept and would exonerate the man-servant mentioned earlier, who had despatched the would-be robbers in such a gruesome manner. Of course the surviving robbers, at the time of the event, would be unlikely to tell anyone about their attempted break-in and perhaps quietly disposed of their comrades' bodies. However, following the removal of the skulls from the farm it is said that they were placed in a 'rockery' at Bradshaw Hall and there they performed 'ornamental service'.

How long this service was rendered isn't known but it is said that when they left their resting place the peace of the farmhouse was once more broken. Presumably further consultation transpired between the landlord and his tenants and it was then decided that the skulls should be returned to the old cheese-room. Albeit this time, the room was to be secured in such a way that no one was able to gain access to the skulls or indeed to be aware of their existence. Only the men who were called to seal off the room by using 'stone and mortar,' may have known what secret was being concealed. [12]

THE HARDCASTLE FAMILY AND BRADSHAW HALL

The farmhouse and the land on which it stood were owned by the Hardcastle family, who had lived in the Bradshaw district for centuries. The Hardcastles' residence was at Bradshaw Hall, which was situated a little over a quarter of a mile north of the then rural village of Bradshaw. The village itself stood two and a half miles north-east from Bolton. It was said of Bradshaw that the village enjoys the curious reputation of possessing 'a church without a steeple, a steeple without a church and the local hostelry is the house without a name!' [13]

The village does indeed have a steeple, or 'tower' as it is presently called, that stands alone in the local churchyard. It is all that remains of a 16th century chapel of ease. Whilst in close proximity to it and standing within the same churchyard, is the church of St. Maxentius.

Although acknowledging that the Timberbottom skulls were possibly the result of an attempted robbery, local author Albert Winstanley, writes about another variation of the skulls' history. He suggests that the skulls could be that of a man and his wife and that the man first killed the woman and then he himself committed suicide. [14]

This suggestion is embellished by Vivienne Rae-Ellis when she writes that the skulls were of two young people who, many years ago, wanted to be married but their union was vehemently opposed by their respective families. Not wishing to be parted from each other in this life, they sought to kill themselves so that they could be together in the next. Since there would have been a scandal if the act were known, it is suggested that all was hushed up and the couples' bodies were secretly buried in ground near to Timberbottom Farm. The skulls were later unearthed during excavations of the ground and taken inside the farmhouse where they were displayed on the mantelpiece. [15]

WRITER'S NOTE:

The suggestion made by Vivienne Rae-Ellis sounds plausible but the evidence is scant. Why were only two skulls found and nothing else? What happened to the remainder of the skeletons? Furthermore, where did the idea originate to suggest that one of the skulls was male and the other female?

HISTORICAL LOCATIONS

The map in photo No 3 shows the location of the three historic buildings that are mentioned in the text. At some time in their history they each housed the infamous Timberbottom Farm skulls. The square shape at the top of the page denotes Turton Tower. The circular shape in the middle of the map locates Bradshaw Hall and the triangular shape at the foot of the page highlights the position of Timberbottom Farm.

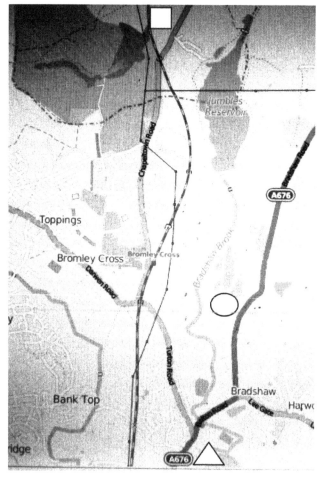

©Open Street Map contributors

Photo No 3 (circa: 2014)
Map showing locations of historical buildings

MR. HARRY PRICE

A clue for a possible answer to these questions is held in the writings of a man named Harry Price. During the 1920s he was best described as a 'psychic detective' and was widely known in spiritualist circles. He had spent much of his adult life researching psychic phenomena and had written some books on the subject. One book of particular note was about the spirit activities at a place called Borley Rectory, in the county of Essex. Around the time that he had written the book, Colonel Henry Marmaduke Hardcastle had inherited Bradshaw Hall, from his late father.

Additionally, he had also inherited, albeit from his tenants, the problem related to the skulls. Whether the Colonel had stumbled across a copy of the book by chance, or whether he had made a conscious effort to procure one, is not known but what is certain is that Colonel Hardcastle read the book and was suitably inspired by its contents. The Colonel decided to write to Harry Price and tell him about the happenings at Timberbottom Farm. The gist of the communication that transpired between the two men is written in Price's own words:

'The case of Timberbottom Farm first attracted my attention in 1929, when accounts of the affair appeared in the Press. This Timberbottom ghost stumps up and down the stairs just as the Shropshire one did, and I read that it often 'stumbled' and knocked things over. The clatter of fire-irons was heard at night, but in the morning nothing appeared out of place. There were loud knockings in the passages, and shufflings would be heard behind closed doors, and on one occasion a woman said she felt 'something' pass her, and go up the stairs. The legend connected with the farm is almost identical with that connected with the Shropshire manor.

19

It is said that a man once murdered a woman at the farm. The reader will remember that the tradition attached to the Shropshire haunting relates how a demented uncle killed his young niece. One cannot help wondering whether men who murder helpless females are doomed to become stumbling Poltergeists when they 'pass over.'

The owner of the property on which Timberbottom Farm is situated happened to read my book on the haunting of Borley Rectory and wrote to me. He is Colonel Henry M. Hardcastle, of Bradshaw Hall, Bolton. In some correspondence that passed between us during November, 1940, the Colonel told me some interesting things about the farm, which has been in the possession of his family for generations.

The Poltergeist, I was informed, has infested the farm for the last 150 years. In addition to the manifestations I have recorded above, the Poltergeist has a knack of opening and closing a certain chest of drawers in a room above the kitchen, in which many tapping sounds occur. Sometimes the cat will follow the taps around the room. The 'visitations' of the Geist are at long intervals: once nine, and at another time, eleven years.

Colonel Hardcastle related to me a remarkable story of two skulls, one male and one female that used to be at the farm. Many years ago, during one of the periodic disturbances, his grandfather suggested, as a possible way of stopping the trouble, that the skulls should be buried in the churchyard. This was done, whereupon the most violent manifestations broke out all over the house.

The Colonel's grandfather could only make a further suggestion that they should be dug up again. This was done and he put them on the family Bible, where they have remained ever since. The woman's skull, about six inches across, he had mounted in silver and placed on a stand. About nine years ago, Colonel Hardcastle accidentally damaged the mounting and took it and the skull to a Manchester silversmith to be repaired. That very day, the most violent disturbances occurred at the farm. These continued incessantly until the skull was restored to its place alongside its male companion on the family Bible. Then all was quiet again for nine years, when a recrudescence of the trouble occurred in the autumn of 1940.

The Colonel has asked me to investigate the case, and perhaps see what a medium can do. I have promised to help when the present War is over as Timberbottom Farm has great possibilities in the way of experimentation. For example, we might induce phenomena by again removing the silver-mounted skull.' [16]

WRITER'S NOTE:

Reflecting upon the correspondence, it is apparent that the Colonel was sufficiently worried by the 'happenings' to warrant contacting Harry Price. Furthermore it is possible that Price's own words, 'The legend connected with the farm is almost identical with that connected with the Shropshire manor' [17] could have induced the Colonel to seek his advice. Considering that the farm had been plagued by disturbances for the best part of 150 years, the Colonel must have rejoiced when he saw in Price's book a chance to resolve the issue. Regrettably, the writer could find no available evidence to suggest that Colonel Hardcastle had ever met with Harry Price.

The 'War' that Price referred to of course, was the Second World War which ended in 1945. Sadly, less than three years later both the Colonel and Harry Price were dead.

It is obvious from the correspondence that Harry Price was already aware of the activities at the farm, since he says that he had read the related newspaper reports of 1929. The Colonel is said to have stated that the skulls were one 'male' and the other 'female' and that they 'used to be at the farm.' From this information it may be deduced that at some date prior to 1940, the skulls had been removed from their enclosed room at the farm. This is assuming of course that they were enclosed and by now were permanently residing at Bradshaw Hall. It may also be observed that the Colonel refers to the skulls as being one male and the other female and it is from his statement, which may have been an assumption on his part, that the idea appears to have taken root. The writer has not seen any written evidence to suggest that the skulls are of a different sex and is unaware if any medical examination has been carried out on them.

The correspondence between the two men concurs that the visitations of the poltergeist would seem to take place at long intervals, one of which was at nine years and another again at eleven years. This statement suggests to the writer that there may well have been interludes of relative peace. It might therefore follow, that any tenant who had moved into the farmhouse, might initially find the surroundings to be peaceful. Then once the peace was disturbed, the tenant would be induced to vacate. This theory might provide a reason why the skulls were at some point taken from the farmhouse and kept at Bradshaw Hall. Any landlord not wishing to lose a good tenant would surely go to such lengths to preserve status quo. However, it may be noted that after the skulls had been taken to the Hall, the disturbances at the farmhouse continued. Faced with a situation like that was it any wonder that the Colonel would wish to seek help?

On December 23 1927, Timberbottom Farm was visited once again. This time by a knocking sound that was said to be impossible to trace. Periodic noises had been heard at the farmhouse as far back as living memory could tell but this latest occurrence was described as being 'unusually disturbing.' It seems that on one particular night the bout of knocking continued for three hours! It was also reported that a dog that belonged to the farm people, was so terrified, that throughout the following day it was quite unapproachable and it wouldn't eat its food until the evening.

Some possible explanations were offered, such as 'practical jokers' or the 'migration of rodents' but the farm people were quite adamant that these were incapable of causing the mysterious knocking. The report suggests that the most likely cause of the disturbance was the 'pulling down of some old adjacent property' and adds that the skulls 'seem to have been lost.' The writer is of the understanding that the skulls at that time, were in safe keeping at the home of Col. Hardcastle, which of course was Bradshaw Hall. However, it could be possible that the tenants of the farm were unaware of this, or it may be possible that the demolition of the 'old adjacent property,' if any, did have some influence on the situation. In any event, irrespective of the causation of the happening, just about a year later, the knocking sounds were heard again.

In December of 1928, the newspaper, Bolton Evening News, reported that the mysterious ghost of Timberbottom Farm had once again been causing its seasonal disturbances and this time almost to the day as the previous year. The first of the latest bout of visitations occurred one evening, when seven people were gathered in the kitchen of the farmhouse and were having what was said to be a 'jolly time'. The gramophone was emitting pleasant sounds and everyone was in 'good spirits.' Suddenly, their peace was disturbed when a 'loud knocking' was heard coming from the nearby passage.

It was almost as if someone was making a complaint about their merry making. When one of the seven stepped forward and opened a door, expecting to find someone on the other side, there was no one there!

Just before dusk on another afternoon, three 'distinct knocks' were heard on the front door. The lady of the farmhouse opened it but the result was as before; there was no one there! A third occurrence and one that is deemed to be the 'most terrifying,' happened when another lady, who also lived in the farmhouse, walked into the house. It was about nine o' clock in the evening and as she entered the house she heard a 'shuffling' sound behind the front door. More or less straight away she felt something pass her and go up the stairs but of course all of this time she saw nothing. Naturally the lady must have been very upset but she remembered that she had a friend who studied such phenomenon. She quickly invited her to come to the house and spend a night with her. Suitably prepared, the two ladies climbed into bed and the writer can only surmise that they must have spent a very uneasy night.

Sometime during the night they heard 'mysterious steps' moving into the bedroom and then suddenly a 'ghostly knocking.' At first the knocking was heard on the foot board, at the base of the bed and then the knocking stopped; but only to start again on the head board. One can only begin to imagine the fear that the ladies must have felt. Of course the invited lady was not entirely without experience of such things and quickly began an attempt to communicate with the 'visitor.' She addressed the 'visitor' which in turn seemed to reply by giving 'systematic knocks' but sadly the lady couldn't understand what may have been said. At the end of the whole traumatic affair she managed to offer an idea that might explain the mysterious occurrence. She suggested that the visitor may be a man and that he had murdered a woman. Furthermore, she believed that the man was now re-enacting the crime.

This latest visitation wasn't to be the last and in a subsequent visit, it was stated that the 'presence' could be heard 'walking up and down the stairs in the night' and that it 'often stumbled and knocked things over.'

On another occasion and also during the night, some members of the household heard a pile of boxes, which stood at the end of a short dark passage, crash over. In the morning, when they went to investigate, strangely as it appeared, the boxes were all in order. At yet another time, in the downstairs room, the fire irons were heard to be sent clattering about but again, in the morning and upon inspection by members of the household, they were found to be intact. [18]

WRITER'S NOTE:

The lady with knowledge of the paranormal, suggested that the 'visitor' could be a man who had murdered his wife and who was re-enacting the crime. Considering that both Harry Price and Colonel Hardcastle must have read the report it may be possible that this is where they acquired their notion that the skulls are one male and the other female.

GHOST AT TIMBERBOTTOM FARM

At the end of the all night vigil it appeared that the psychic lady had achieved some modicum of success. For the following eleven years there was comparative quiet at Timberbottom Farm, until that is, the night of Friday, October 27th 1939.

The cloudless sky was filled with stars and the moon shone brightly. Shortly before eleven o' clock, the tenants of the farmhouse, Mr. and Mrs. John Heywood, was aroused from slumber. They could hear loud noises which came from the room down stairs and they made them out to be the sound of doors opening and shutting, along with drawers being 'pulled out' and then 'closed again.' It was all as if someone was searching for something.

They felt sure someone was inside the house, especially when they heard the sound of 'heavy footsteps' walking up the stairs; although surprisingly no one attempted to enter their room.

A lodger named Tom Lomas, together with his wife, who had a room on the same level, also heard the disturbance, which prompted some action. The two men met on the stairs, with Tom Lomas carrying a torch and John Heywood armed with a stick. When they entered the lower level of the house, fully expecting to find someone waiting for them, there was no one there! However, although there was nothing visible, the noises continued and lasted for 'about two hours.' After listening to the sounds and yet seeing nothing to cause them, the nocturnal 'visitor' was finally heard to lift the latch of the front door and walk down the flagged path, outside the house.

One can only imagine the consternation that was experienced by the two guardians of the house, when some fifteen minutes later, the 'visitor' returned and was heard to be making a further search of the room. By now the time was around four in the morning and the household members were thoroughly tired out, in fact, so much so that they fell asleep. During the course of the next day or two, it was not entirely unexpected when the Lomas couple announced that they were leaving the farm. They had lodged there for the past eight months but Mrs. Lomas, who, after her experience, was said to look 'frightened and ill,' couldn't find the will to stay another night.

As for the Heywood couple; they had experienced similar happenings before. John Heywood had actually been born at the farm and his family had spent the best part of a hundred years there. John had grown up with the periodic 'visitations' but he had to admit that the most recent visit was 'powerful.' He said that he and Tom Lomas were obliged to investigate when they heard the intensity of the sounds. But when they walked into the living room they found 'not the slightest sign of any upset.' Both the men found this most surprising and John Heywood went on to say;

"Doors and windows and drawers were all secure just as they'd been left. Even the cat was sitting in a chair at the fireplace. We went through every room and found all in order; yet judging by t'row we'd had you'd have thought a furniture remover was in!" [19]

Mrs. Heywood of course was still in her bed when the disturbance was taking place and described the 'visit' from her point of view. She said that she had never believed in the existence of ghosts or met evidences of them before she lived at the farm. She really thought that the noises were caused by burglars. She described the noise like 'somebody was lifting doors off their hinges' and she also noted two strange things. One was that the 'visitor' walked into only one of the bedrooms, which was small and unoccupied. The other was that on the last journey that it made, whilst walking up the stairs, 'it seemed to pause halfway up for about ten minutes.' It seems that the 'visitor' walked up and down the stairs several times and each time sounding like a 'heavily-built man, wearing big boots.'

Mrs. Heywood confirmed that there were no sounds of groaning, moaning or even chain rattling and she had never seen any sort of manifestation. However, she pointed out that "It's as powerful as any strong man and it's there without a doubt." Mr. Heywood was listening to his wife's account and when she had finished he nodded approvingly, saying, "It's been there since my grandfather's day and it'll remain when this place has been knocked down." [20]

WRITER'S NOTE:

The owner of Bradshaw Hall assured a reporter of the Bolton Journal and Guardian newspaper, that the skulls were in no way disturbed on the night of the happenings and that they continued to rest in their usual place, which was on top of the family's Holy Bible, where they had stood for seventy years.

MR. ARTHUR CLIFFORD AND MR. JACK FALON

In the year 1995, Mr. Arthur Clifford, of Rutland House, Mill view, Bridgeman Street, Bolton, wrote to the Bolton Evening News about his recollection of the Timberbottom Farm skulls:

> "Our milk man was James Heywood of Timberbottom Farm and when I was eight years old, in 1922, I remember Mrs Heywood delivering the milk and telling my mother that the cat and dog had run off. The previous night she had heard knocking and scratching at the door and thought someone had brought the animals back. When she opened the door, nothing was there, but she heard footsteps go past her across the room and up the stairs." [21]

Mr. Clifford remembered hearing it said that whenever the skulls at Bradshaw Hall were separated, the disturbances happened again. He recalled that some time after the occurrence, it was discovered that Colonel Hardcastle had sent one of the skulls away for remounting. The smaller of the two skulls was mounted on a silver stand and in some way this had been damaged which necessitated Colonel Hardcastle to send it to Manchester for repair. [22]

There was another memory from later years that Mr. Clifford shared, which involved his friend, Jack Falon. His friend happened to be courting a maid who worked at Bradshaw Hall and one night, by way of having some fun, she dared him to sit at the banqueting table, which was in the Colonel's trophy room. There in the dark and with a skull placed at each end of the table, Jack Falon was told to wait. After only a minute of sitting there, he felt "the hair on the back of his neck stand up" said Mr. Clifford. Then without further ado he "shot out of the room like a scared rabbit." The maid caught up with her man friend and laughingly she apologised saying that "it took a brave man even to attempt it." She then went back to the trophy room to placate the troubled spirits. [23]

MR. THOMAS CROMPTON

It seems that the maid was not the only person to have a laugh at the expense of the skulls, as Mr. Thomas Crompton, of Stanworth Avenue, Breightmet, confirms. He explained to a reporter of the Bolton Evening News, that during the 1940s he and his pal, Dick Greenhalgh, were gainfully employed as decorators. On one occasion they were doing some decorating at Bradshaw Hall, whilst the owner, Colonel Hardcastle, was at Southport convalescing, following a recent operation. Keeping a watchful eye on things, whilst he was away, was the elderly housekeeper, but she failed to notice when the two decorators decided to have a bit of fun.

Thomas Crompton had an old book containing the story of the skulls and having read it arranged to move one of them. At that time the skulls were kept on top of a Holy Bible that was placed in the Chapel. Thomas took one of the skulls and moved it to the Morning Room, where it was left for about a week. Unfortunately though Thomas had to admit, that "contrary to the story; nothing happened" and so he returned the skull to the Chapel.

The newspaper reporter, whilst wishing to put a damper on the decorator's apparent 'victory' over the power of the skulls, made a suggestion. He said that since there was no activity taking place at the Hall, it was most probably happening at the farm. That is where it would be expected to happen but of course Thomas and his friend weren't to know that.

There was another incident that Mr. Crompton remembered from his working life, which he also shared with the newspaper reporter. He said that there was a time when he and his workmates were working at Turton Tower, having been hired to remove some old panelling from the walls. It was during this period that they devised a new idea to have some fun.

Thomas mentioned that one of his pals had got two very old coins in some change, which he had been given at his local public house. The coins were placed down the back of the panelling and the lads waited for the arrival of Mr. Reginald Dart, who was the Surveyor for Turton Council. As the panelling was removed the two coins dropped to the floor and were spotted by Mr. Dart. "Good heavens" he declared, "see what I have found" and then he quickly put them into his pocket! [24]

MRS. BRENDA THORPE

Mrs. Marjorie Horrocks (nee Lomas), who lived at Tinturn Avenue, Tonge Moor, Bolton, also spoke to a journalist of the Bolton Evening News. Her account added to the growing collection of stories, that related to Timberbottom Farm. She and her family had lived at the farm during the 1930s when it would seem that it was split into two sections. The Lomas family had lived in one of the sections, whilst Mr. and Mrs. Heywood lived in the other. She related an incident that she remembered from a day during the 1930s, when her mother was alone in their house, since her father was at work doing his job as a bus conductor.

Her mother heard noises and shortly after felt 'a funny sensation'. Very soon after this she saw a 'lady walking' and pots and pans were 'inexplicably thrown about the room'. At this point Mrs. Horrocks' mother fainted and had to be taken to hospital. She later learned that her mother's hair had changed to grey overnight, although she was only in her late 20s. When her mother recovered from her shock and was eventually taken home, Mrs. Horrocks said that her mother would never talk about the incident again. She also recalls that some time later a priest was called to visit the farm with a view to performing an exorcism. [25]

MR. ALBERT WINSTANLEY

Mr. Albert Winstanley, of Bradshaw Brow, Bradshaw, was another who wrote to the Bolton Evening News to say that the back door to his cottage and its garden, immediately faced Timberbottom Farm before its demolition.

"I knew the last occupants, Mr. and Mrs. Heywood, very well indeed and often visited them at the farm for a chat. I knew the mantelpiece where the skulls were placed after they had been taken from Bradshaw Brook. Both Mr. and Mrs. Heywood, however, were afraid to talk about their experiences and though I wanted to spend a night in the farm they would not allow me to do so. Mr. Heywood was a down to earth Lancashire man, who liked a flutter on the horses. Once I offered to place a bet on for him with a bookie that I knew, and after this he called most days, unknown to his wife, with his 'stake.'

Mrs. Heywood once told my wife of when, in the first days at the farm, she was 'shaken' in bed, and of how she almost jumped out of the window in her fright. There was a day when I was at work, when Mr. Heywood came rushing up to my garden in his nightshirt, shouting some b..... has moved those b..... skulls at the Tower. [It transpired that a cleaner at Turton Tower had been dusting them.]

On another occasion, a near neighbour was helping Mr. Heywood with some decorating and they were hanging wallpaper at the top of the stairs. My neighbour told me he 'sensed' something passing between him and Mr. Heywood and he remarked, "I've suddenly gone cold!" to which Mr. Heywood replied, "Aye, an' I've gone bloody cold too!" [26]

31

Photo No 4 (circa: 2012)
Stone lintel from Timberbottom Farm

Photo No 5 (circa: 2012)
Date on the lintel from Timberbottom Farm

At the end of the 1950s it was decided to demolish Timberbottom Farm and clear the site for the purpose of erecting a housing estate. Mr. Albert Winstanley became concerned when the contractors started work on the nearby coach-house. It stood together with the stables and the facing smithy, on the opposite side of the lane to Timberbottom Farm. Over the doorway of the coach-house and the stables was a stone lintel which was embossed with the year 1683. [See Photos No 4 and No 5]

Mister Winstanley contacted the authorities at Turton Tower to see if the stone lintel could be preserved as a part of local history. Following some discussion with the powers that be, a man was sent along with a wheel barrow with the hope of collecting the stone. The man soon realised that it would need more than himself to lift it and certainly more than a wheelbarrow to transport it. Happily, the lintel eventually found its way to the Museum and it can be seen today placed on the grass verge at the base of the original peel Tower. [27]

TIMBERBOTTOM FARM SKULLS

The stone lintel wasn't the only item that travelled from Timberbottom Farm to find a new home at Turton Tower. There were also the two skulls that had reputedly been the cause of many disturbances at the farm. The reader will recall that the disturbances had been experienced periodically for more than a century and that the last resting place for them had been at Bradshaw Hall.

In 1949, as Bradshaw Hall was being demolished, many of its antiquities were taken to Turton Tower, together with the skulls. Today the skulls are placed inside a secured glass-panelled cabinet and are displayed in the Tower's Ashworth Room. One of them is sizeable in that it consists of most of the cranium and forehead but is minus the facial parts, which are the eye sockets and nose, as well as the jaw bone.

The second skull is practically none existent and can best be compared to the half of an average sized cocoanut. The periphery of its broken edge is trimmed with silver. It is mounted in an up-turned position atop a silver stand which looks like the lower part of a candlestick. [See Photos No 6 & 7]

In accordance with tradition, they are kept on top of a Holy Bible that once belonged to the Hardcastle family.

Tradition has it that if the skulls are separated for any reason, then the mysterious disturbances shall start again. It is said that the smaller portion of a skull is that of a female, while the larger relic is male but the writer wonders how that is so. As far as the writer is aware the skulls have never been examined by medical experts. Therefore, it may be due to the physical size of the smaller skull, that has perpetuated the thought that it is female. It should also be mentioned that the larger relic has what appears to be a crack in what might be described as the forehead.

The crack extends for three or four inches from its front edge to its upper central area and may have been caused by a blow from a sharp instrument such as a sword or even an axe. There is also an oval-shaped area, looking rather like a large vaccination mark, which sits adjacent to the crack. [See Photo No 7] Of course there is no evidence to support these suggestions. Considering their age and the rough treatment they may have received during the passage of time, anything is possible.

Photo No 6 (circa: 2014)
The Timberbottom farm skulls

Photo No 7 (circa: 2014)
The Timberbottom farm skulls placed on a Holy Bible

Photo No 8 (circa: 2014)
Mr Ian Briggs at Bradshaw Brook (Labby's Hole)

One version of the skulls' story is that they were found around the year 1750, either in the Bradshaw Brook or dug up on its bank. Photo No 8 was taken near to where they were said to be found, at a place called 'Labby's Hole'.

BRADSHAW HALL

Photo No 9 (circa: 1940)
Bradshaw Hall

The once magnificent Bradshaw Hall is portrayed in Photograph No 9. It was home to the Hardcastle family until its last owner, Colonel Henry M. Hardcastle, died in 1948. In the following year it was agreed to demolish the most part of the Hall, except for the 17th century porch and the modern north-west wing. The latter being erected by the late Thomas Hardcastle during the years 1880-1882.

Legend has it that in a will of a former occupant they were to be preserved as an example of early architecture. However, another version has it that they were left because plans were afoot to develop the area into a leisure park and the porch was to be a central feature. A semi-circular beaded doorway forms the porch entrance. This is framed with coarse Tuscan columns on pedestals, that support an entablature with spiked finials. The coat of arms of the Bradshaw family are carved in stone and placed above the doorway.

If the reader looks carefully at the bottom right-hand corner of the photograph, two female figures can be seen who appear to be clothed in maid's uniforms.

The writer wonders if one of them was the maid that was courting Jack Falon, who was mentioned earlier in this story. At the top left-hand corner of the photograph, a part section of a mill chimney can be seen standing ominously in the back ground. Built in the year 1848, the 160 feet tall chimney belonged to the Bradshaw bleach-works. The works consisted of a conglomeration of buildings of which one was a boiler house, with its attendant chimney stack.

Photo No 10 (circa: 1951)
The Bradshaw Bleach Works

The works complex was built next to the left bank of a river that was known as Bradshaw Brook. This was the same river that flowed passed Timberbottom Farm, where it was said that the remains of two human skulls were found. Photo No 10 illustrates the extent of the works and in the centre of the image can be seen the 160 feet tall chimney.

Just over a hundred years after it was built, the chimney was demolished but the demolition didn't go quite according to plan. In fact there was a suggestion that some supernatural influence occurred on that day and details of the event are described later in this narrative.

There is mention of property having been built at Bradshaw, on the site of what was Bradshaw Hall, as early as 1074AD. The Bradshaw family and their direct descendents owned the site on which they built a Hall and lived there from the year 1250AD onwards. At the time of the English Civil War the owner of Bradshaw Hall was a John Bradshaw, who was born in 1585 and died in 1665. He had been a Gentleman of Grays Inn, London, in the year 1602. He was also a Justice of the Peace, a Commissioner for Recuscancy and High Sheriff of Lancashire.

Soon after the Reformation, the Bradshaws adopted the Protestant form of worship and thereafter were known for their Calvinist and Presbyterian convictions. In the year 1694, John Bradshaw, who was the eighth in succession of that name to live at Bradshaw Hall, sold the buildings and the right to bear the ancient Bradshaw coat-of-arms. He left the area soon after and was never heard of again.

Some miles away at Wybersley Hall, in the County of Cheshire, lived Henry Bradshawe and his wife Catherine. It was there that they began a branch of the family tree. In the year 1602, they produced a son whom they named John Bradshawe. It may be noted that this branch of the extended Bradshaw family had adopted the letter 'e' at the end of their surname. The Cheshire born John Bradshawe, studied law and in 1627 was called to the bar, after which he built up a lucrative career. At the time when Oliver Cromwell's Parliament put King Charles I on trial for treason, it was John Bradshawe who was the presiding judge. He was also one of the many who put his signature to the King's death warrant. This act resulted in him being known thereafter as John Bradshawe, the 'Regicide.'

Tradition has it that John Bradshawe actually signed the death warrant whilst he was temporarily resident at the Bradshaw Hall in Lancashire. There is also mention that as a younger man and once again whilst resident at Bradshaw Hall, he had an early encounter with the King.

However, there is scant evidence, if at all any, to show that these stories are true. That being said, it is interesting to recount the legends that connect John Bradshawe with Lancashire's Bradshaw Hall.

GHOSTLY SIGHTINGS AT BRADSHAW HALL

In 1945, Alderman George Harry Ashworth wrote a booklet containing two stories that he considered to be questionable. However, he stated that they were too well known by persons living at that time, to be dismissed as being of no importance. He writes that one of the many antiquities that were bequeathed to Turton Tower Museum, was a baby's cradle. It is made from wood and having the year 1630 carved into one of its end pieces. The cradle is described as being one of the original pieces of furniture that belonged to Bradshaw Hall. Tradition has it that when the cradle was at Bradshaw Hall, it was known to rock of its own accord. Similarly, since it has taken up residence at Turton Tower, there too it has been known to rock.

One version of the rocking-cradle story takes place at the time of the Stuart's reign. It appears that a daughter of the then owner of Bradshaw Hall, who was 'idolised' by both her father and her brother, was betrayed by her lover. At that point, the girl's brother, who was normally a quiet and studious sort of lad, was fused with revenge. His one ambition in life became the need to avenge his sister's suffering. One night, about mid-night and whilst unable to sleep, the brother was pacing the terrace outside the Hall. Suddenly he saw the figure of a man 'muffled in a dark cloak.' The figure was attempting to climb through a 'gap in the lane' and afterwards succeeded in entering the garden.

The intruder stealthily made his way towards the window of the young girl's bedroom and then stopped. Picking up a hand full of gravel he threw it at the window, whilst hoping to arouse the girl's attention. Unfortunately for him, at that moment the cloud-filled sky parted and revealed the moon.

It was shining in all its brilliance. As the moonlight reflected from his face, the presence of the visitor was instantly exposed. Like a cat having stalked a mouse, the young Bradshaw(e) pounced on the man and threw him to the ground. The man lay prostrate on the gravel, whilst young Bradshaw(e) drew his sword. He was about to run him through when the man cried, "Villain, would'st thou murder thy King?" Taken aback by this outburst, the young Bradshaw(e) froze. As if in suspended animation both hunter and prey looked at each other. Suddenly they heard a 'piercing shriek' emanate from the direction of the girl's bedroom window.

The spell was broken and their gaze was instantly averted. The doting brother acted as though he had forgotten what he was about to do and instinctively ran towards the house. As for the intruder; he quickly picked himself up and made his getaway. When the young girl's bedroom was entered she was found to be dying. She was heard to murmur the name of her lover. Ever since that time, according to the story, when it is a moonlit night, the ghost of the unhappy girl is to be seen looking from her bedroom window. [28]

WRITER'S NOTE:

The story can't be verified but it raises a few questions.

Is it possible that the girl died from a heart attack after seeing her paramour about to be murdered?

The suggestion that follows is that the girl was rocking the cradle before she was 'shocked' to death. Perhaps she continues to do so in her spiritual state.

The writer wonders why the girl would be rocking a cradle. Is it possible that it contained her child and that the father had come to see them both?

Curiously, the year 1630 carved in one end of the cradle, is the year when the son of Charles I was born.

MR. THOMAS HARDCASTLE

Mr. Thomas Hardcastle J.P., who was the owner of Bradshaw Hall, died unexpectedly on September 27th 1902. His death followed a brief illness at his home of Blaston Hall, in Leicestershire. His remains were conveyed to Bradshaw Hall for his admirers to be allowed to attend a funeral service. Afterwards he was taken to Horninghold, Market Harborough, Leicester, for interment. His second son, Colonel Henry Marmaduke Hardcastle, (Born. 23-03-1871) took up residence at Bradshaw Hall following his father's funeral. He continued to live there until his own death on 13th May 1948.

Colonel Hardcastle was educated at Charterhouse and the Manchester College of Technology and at the age of eighteen he assisted his father at Bradshaw Bleach Works. Together they developed new methods to improve the production processes. He later joined the Bolton Squadron of the Duke of Lancaster's Own Yeomanry. When the Boer War began, he travelled to South Africa with the Squadron as a subaltern. During his time of service he rose to the rank of Major. Upon his return to Bradshaw he found that the Bleach works had been absorbed into the Bleachers' Association.

When his father died he became a Director of the Association but took no active part in the management of the Bradshaw works. He later became a member of the British Cotton Association and then, in 1904, he was appointed a member of the Bolton County Bench, in the role of Senior Magistrate and was also a Deputy Lieutenant of the County. Fishing and shooting were among his pastimes with some occasional big game hunting. He was a senior member of the Holcombe Hunt, which he first joined when he was only nine years old and was its Master from 1906 to 1919.

During the First World War he saw active service and during which he raised a second line of Yeomanry. He later served as a military governor in Ireland having the power of a Commander-In-Chief. He was demobilised in 1919 and at the request of Lord Derby re-formed the Duke of Lancaster's Own

Yeomanry. On his retirement in 1920 he became Honorary Colonel of the Regiment and represented it at the Coronation of King George VI. [29] This was the Colonel Hardcastle who had contacted Harry Price, the psychic investigator. Also, on his death he bequeathed lots of his personal antiquities to the Turton Tower Museum.

Photo No 11 (circa: 1920s)
Colonel H.M. Hardcastle

THE PRIESTLY GHOST OF BRADSHAW HALL

Alderman G. H. Ashworth's booklet states that the rocking of the cradle and the ghostly appearance of the young girl, were not the only paranormal happenings at Bradshaw Hall. Another he mentions is about a certain Colonel Hambridge, who about the year 1930, travelled from Scotland to visit the owner of the Hall. At that time, the existence of a ghostly priest was common knowledge amongst the locals but it hadn't been seen for many years. One evening when the two gentlemen were seated at a dining table and about to enjoy a meal, Colonel Hambridge voiced an observation. He remarked that he thought it unusual there was only two places laid at the table, especially since there was another guest at the Hall.

When pressed for an explanation regarding the other guest, the Colonel explained that he had seen a 'form.' He said it was clad in long raiment and moved slowly and silently down the passage. The puzzled host pondered over the description of the 'form' and then arrived at a conclusion. He suddenly exclaimed, "You must have seen the ghost!"

The host then suggested that the 'form' must have been making its way towards the Stone Hall in which stood a large fireplace. He added that there was a secret passage inside its chimney and that it connected with a hiding chamber, which was situated on the first floor above. The host assured the Colonel that the ghost must have been heading for that place. In summing up the story, Mr. Ashworth states that no cause was given for the surprise appearance and no mention of it has been made since. [30]

Vivienne Rae-Ellis in her book, *True Ghost Stories of our time,* offers another version of this story. She maintains that a Mrs Irene Heaton (nee Deakin), was a close friend of Colonel Hardcastle and often visited him at the Hall. She had the following story to tell about the ghost. She remembers that a friend of her parents, who she calls Major Ryan (an anonymous name), was an army officer and living in Scotland at that time. She says he was invited to join Colonel Hardcastle at the Hall for a spot of shooting.

Major Ryan arrived late one day, tired and travel-stained and was immediately shown up to his room. A hot bath was prepared for him and he was invited to change, before joining his host for dinner. As he made his way towards the bathroom, along an oak-panelled and dimly lit passage, he saw what he took to be a fellow guest. The guest was dressed in a robe and entered the bathroom before him. Feeling somewhat cheated out of his much desired bath, he returned to his room. There he waited with the bedroom door ajar. He hoped to catch a glimpse of the unwanted bather on his return journey.

At length his patience ran out and once more he went down the passage to investigate. On arrival at the bathroom he found it to be empty. Except for the water-filled bath, which by now was barely warm. Not wishing to waste any more time, or water for that matter, he quickly bathed and changed his clothes. As the Major, who was freshly attired, eventually entered the dining hall, he saw the Colonel standing in front of a roaring fire. He was holding a welcoming drink in his hand.

The two officers were soon engrossed in conversation, during which the Major explained why he was delayed for dinner. He put the blame on the other guest who had robbed him of his earlier bath. The Colonel expressed surprise and explained that there was no other guest. He quickly showed the Major the two places set out at the dining table. Feeling perplexed the Major accepted the Colonel's invitation to sit at the table. They awaited the arrival of the soup.

In mid-conversation the Major suddenly caught sight of a robed figure standing behind the Colonel's chair. "Look, there he is!" exclaimed the Major and pointed to the apparition. The Colonel instantly turned his head blurting out the words, "Where? Who?" but saw nothing. A second or two later the Major shouted again, "There! Standing behind your chair now!" Once more the Colonel turned his head only to see nothing. Presently, as if he had heard a spoken joke and had just understood the punch line, he began to chuckle.

"I never can see him! Much as I would like to!" said the Colonel. "It's our monk, you know! I find it so disappointing that I have not got the gift of second sight! You would have seen him upstairs since the bathroom used to be a priest hole. He often appears there, and on the staircase, but never for me, sad to say!"

Mrs. Heaton explained that Colonel Hardcastle had told her personally that he would have given his right-arm to see the monk. She said that at one time he had considered having the monk exorcised but since he was doing no harm; save for giving the occasional guest a near heart attack, he let him alone.

Mrs Heaton recalled that during her lifetime there had been several sightings of the ghostly monk. One of them in particular, was when a fancy dress party was held at the Hall. A lady guest, who happened to be standing on the staircase caught sight of the ghostly monk and instantly fainted. Her dilemma created quite a stir but later she became the heroine of the party. Apparently, after the excitement had calmed down a certain wit was heard to remark, "She was the life and the monk was the soul of the party!" [31]

BRADSHAW BLEACH-WORKS

Photo No 12 (circa: 1989)
The remains of Bradshaw Hall porch

Aside from the stories that relate to the Timberbottom farmhouse and those of Bradshaw Hall, there is a curious sequel that relates to the Bradshaw bleach-works and in particular to its boiler-house chimney. The bleach-works was closed in 1963 and some years later in 1989, the chimney was felled. The site was cleared to make way for a housing development. The base of the chimney was temporarily supported by some wooden props before they were set alight.

After some time they burnt through and the chimney began to descend. It was supposed to drop out of harm's way and on to an open area of land. Unexpectedly, as it began to topple, it 'suddenly twisted' and crashed on to the preserved Bradshaw Hall porch. An eye witness, Mr. Jim Francis, who was at that time Chairman of the Turton Committee of the Civic Trust, exclaimed, "I couldn't believe my eyes!" He went on to say, "It looked to be dropping where it was intended, but it suddenly seemed to twist." [32]

MR. PETER GREENHALGH

Mr. Peter Greenhalgh of Stonesteads Way, Bromley Cross, expressed his view about the felling of the bleach works chimney:

> "Bradshaw Hall had stood adjacent to the bleach-works until it was demolished in 1949; apart from its main entrance porch that was left standing as some kind of memorial to the Hall and to those who had lived there. According to eye witness accounts the old chimney at first fell in the direction intended, which was well away from the nearby structures. However, it suddenly twisted as it fell; its direction changed and it crashed onto the porch. I suppose it is true to say that the chimney was just as much a memorial to the bleach-works as the porch was to the Hall. The latter had been the home of the Hardcastle family for many years and the coat of arms of Thomas Hardcastle (1836-1902) was carved over the door inside the porch. Thus the porch was a memorial to him and his family as well as to his old home. The works had been owned by the Hardcastles, so the old chimney was a kind of memorial to them. Now, with an almost uncanny twist, defeating the best efforts of those felling the chimney, both it and the porch now lay in ruins." [33]

46

MR. J. LOMAX

Mr J. Lomax, of Glazedale Street, Tonge Moor, later felt compelled to write to the Bolton Evening News about his experience. He wrote that he had been originally asked to quote for the felling of the chimney but had failed to get the contract. In his letter to the newspaper he described what happened when he first went to look at the site:

"I went one evening at about 7.30 to look at the site and chimney. Standing between the chimney and the porch I suddenly got a very uneasy feeling that someone was watching. The chimney was tall and the base square, built in stone, with a large hole in the south-west side.

I was about 60 to 70 yards from it when I saw a figure standing in the opening at the base. I thought it was someone walking a dog. I walked towards the chimney and much to my astonishment the figure started to fade.

At this point I suddenly got a premonition of the chimney hitting the porch. Sometime later I was told that I hadn't got the contract. I told the site agent about my experience and what might happen to the chimney. The rest is history! But who was the figure in the base of the chimney? Was it the ghost of Thomas Hardcastle?" [34]

BRADSHAW HALL PORCH

Photo No 13 (circa: 2014)
The Bradshaw Hall porch

All that remains of the once grand Bradshaw Hall is the memorial porch that is shown in Photo No 13. Standing like a silent sentinel, the memorial appears to be guarding the new housing cluster, that was built on the reclaimed bleach-works site.

A year after the original porch was demolished by the 'freak' accident, the present porch was reconstructed at a cost of more than £50,000. It was said that the rebuilding was tantamount to an 'intricate historical jigsaw puzzle' because the builders had to sift through the rubble and separate the debris of both the chimney and the porch. [35]

A semi-circular beaded doorway forms the porch entrance. It is framed with coarse Tuscan columns that are mounted on pedestals. They in turn support an entablature with spiked finials. The coat of arms of the Bradshaw family, in the shape of a small shield, can be seen carved in stone and placed above the arch of the doorway.

A modern blue-coloured sign is fixed to the stonework above the entrance arch and reads: 'This Jacobean porch is all that remains of Bradshaw Hall, the home of the Bradshaw family who lived here from the 12th to the 18th century. Later occupants, the Lomaxes and Hardcastles developed the bleach-works on the site.-Bolton Civic Trust 1986.'

The blue coloured sign appears to be an oddity in itself since the year of '1986' is printed on it and yet the porch was demolished in 1989 and later rebuilt in 1990. The explanation of the oddity is that the porch was in a poor state of repair by the year of 1986. That was largely due to a combined assault by vandals and the elements.

Funding was eventually found and the porch was restored before the end of the year. The blue-coloured sign was made to mark the event but the unveiling ceremony only took place the following year. The sign, along with a small stone coat of arms, was retrieved from the rubble of the demolished chimney and reinstated to the rebuilt porch.

WRITER'S NOTE:

Is it possible that some paranormal influence was present on the day the chimney was felled? The statements from some of the eye witnesses would seem to suggest that it was.

Mr Lomax stated that prior to the chimney being felled he visited the site and although no one was around, he got "a very uneasy feeling that someone was watching". Sometime later he saw a figure, which, much to his astonishment, "started to fade!"

Then there was Mr Jim Francis who on the day of the felling said, "I couldn't believe my eyes" - "It looked to be dropping where it was intended, but it suddenly seemed to twist."

After digesting these statements, the writer is of the opinion that something of a supernatural nature, could have influenced the events of that day.

TURTON TOWER

Photo No 14 (circa: 2013)
Turton Tower with the yew trees on the right

SIR LEES KNOWLES (1857 – 1928)

From about the year 1809 through to 1835, the Tower building was occupied as a farm-house and was also used as a corn-mill. The structure suffered as a result of this and in the year 1835, James Kay purchased the Tower and proceeded to restore it as a home for himself and his family.

In 1890, he sold Turton Tower and his various farms to two wealthy spinsters. For a time they leased the Tower to the Rigg family, who were local mill owners. In 1903 Sir Lees Knowles, the son of the great Lancashire mining family, became the new owner. At the time of the purchase, Sir Lees owned coalmines in Agecroft, Little Lever, Clifton, Pendlebury, and also in Turton, which collectively employed more than 3500 men. In 1894, on the death of John, his father, he succeeded to the chairmanship of Andrew Knowles & sons, coal mines and also to many large properties and estates in the region.

In 1899, he was appointed as Honorary Colonel of the 3rd Volunteer Battalion of the Lancashire Fusiliers, which he supported from his own funds. During the Anglo-Boer War of 1899-1902 he offered 'his' volunteer battalion to the British Forces in the Cape Colony, of South Africa, whom he would arm and equip at his own expense. By so doing, he was later to be known as 'the armchair colonel.'

Photo No 15
Colonel Sir Lees Knowles

The Lancashire Fusiliers distinguished themselves in a battle at Spion Kop (Hill) in the province of Natal, South Africa. The result caused Col. Knowles to campaign for the recognition of their bravery. Eventually the War Office conferred three honours on them. In addition the City Council erected the Boer War Monument in Salford to honour their action. Finally in 1903, for his contribution to the war effort, Col. Knowles was created a baron. Many of his ancestors, who lived in the village of Quarlton, are buried at Chapeltown, in St. Anne's Church graveyard. It is thought this may have influenced him to purchase Turton Tower.

By 1905 his political career was at an end and he concentrated on running his mines. Then in 1915, he married Lady Nina Ogilvie-Grant. By the time of the General Strike of 1926, the former great company of Andrew Knowles and Sons had ceased to exist. When Sir Lees Knowles died, in 1928, his personal fortune was assessed at around £227,000. After his death Lady Knowles chose to live at her other house in Pendlebury. In 1930 she offered Turton Tower to the City of Manchester. The offer was declined and so she presented the Tower to Turton Urban District Council, for the benefit of the people of Turton.

Turton's Urban District Council wasted no time in occupying the Tower. They used its Drawing Room as their Council Chamber and the Dining Room as a Committee Room. One notable Council member was Alderman George Harry Ashworth. He worked diligently throughout the years he spent with the Council, to have part of the Tower converted into a museum. He even donated £1000 of his own money which helped to bring this about. He is remembered today by having a bedroom on the second floor of the Tower named after him. The Tower was officially opened as a museum by the Rt. Hon., the Earl of Derby, M.C., J.P., Lord Lieutenant of Lancashire, on Wednesday the 25th June 1952.

Photo No 16 (circa: 1926)
Alderman G. H. Ashworth

PARANORMAL ACTIVITY AT TURTON TOWER

Considering the age of Turton Tower and the fact that it has had numerous owners, it would surely warrant the possibility that some ghostly presence might exist. It so happens that a number of supernatural occurrences have been recorded throughout the years. The earliest account of which the writer is aware, happened during the reign of Queen Victoria. It is stated that during the lifetime of the first Mr. Kay, a lady guest had a ghostly encounter, whilst visiting the Tower.

THE SILK-CLAD LADY OF TURTON TOWER

Late one night, as the lady guest was 'passing from the billiards room,' which was situated on the second floor, she became terrified when she heard the sound of 'rustling silk.' It seemed to be proceeding towards her from the direction of the large wooden staircase. The sound grew progressively louder as it drew closer to where she was standing but there was nothing visible for the lady to see. Then, as the sound reached a climax, whatever was there succeeded in touching her garment.

It immediately passed by her and continued its journey 'in the direction of the disused dungeon.' The guest concluded that the sound of the 'rustling silk,' was similar to that made from a dress, that might have been worn by a lady from an earlier era. Because of this association in the mind of the perceiver, the Tower phantom was considered to be a 'silk-clad lady.'

Hours later, having come to terms with her frightening encounter, the brave lady chose to continue her stay at the Tower. She subsequently spent a lot of her time trying to convince sceptics to believe what had happened. But the shock that she had experienced wouldn't be her last; although she wasn't to know that until a few days later.

As everyone was peacefully sleeping, at around four o' clock in the morning, suddenly there was 'a mysterious and terrible rumbling' noise that dramatically awakened the whole household. It was said that the Tower shook to its 'very foundations.'

The lady guest, who had previously experienced the ghostly encounter, was sleeping in a 'huge canopied bed' which at that time was situated next to the billiard room. The lady must have been beside herself at that moment, as she was convinced that the huge bed actually lifted off the bedroom floor!

One can only imagine the buzz that must have taken place in the Tower that morning and throughout the remainder of the day. Everyone would have had their own version of events to tell but the writer feels sure, that none would have been as graphic, as that expressed by the lady guest!

It was only the following day that some understanding of events came into play. There happened to be a visit from the local postman, who was carrying his usual delivery of mail but it was his passing casual remark that managed to upset the proverbial apple cart. As he handed over the letters he lazily asked, "Has anyone heard anything about the earthquake of the previous night?" [36]

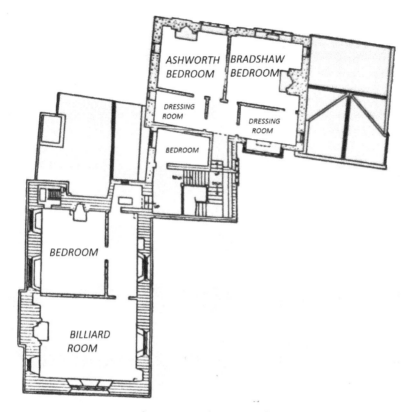

Photo No 17 (circa:1911)
Top floor plan of Turton Tower

Photo No 17 illustrates the top floor plan of Turton Tower.

In the sketch plan can be seen the layout for a billiard room and a bedroom.

The passage outside the billiard room was where Mr Kay's lady guest heard the rustling sound of silk as it brushed passed her.

The adjacent bedroom was where Doris Walker slept on the night that she frightened away the unwelcome visitors to the Tower.

At the top right of the sketch are two large bedrooms with adjacent dressing rooms.

The bedrooms are named 'Ashworth' (left) and 'Bradshaw' (right)

THE 'BOGGART' OF TURTON TOWER

Mr. Ben Brierley, who was a popular Lancashire writer, once gave an account in his periodic 'Journal' about a 'boggart' that was feared to have taken up residence at Turton Tower. The consensus of opinion was that one wing of the Tower was considered to be haunted and none of the servants could be prevailed upon to sleep there. During the night people would lie in their beds and listen to 'an occasional bumping sound' on the main staircase, which sounded as if someone was 'going up and down' the stairs. To make matters worse the noise could be heard every night around midnight and would continue at short intervals.

For a long time the mystery of the nightly visitation remained unsolved but eventually an explanation was found. It transpired that a rodent had visited a store room in the upper reaches of the building and had nibbled a hole in a sack of potatoes that it found there. The resourceful rat had industriously rolled a number of potatoes from the sack and had managed to send them bouncing down the staircase. The mysterious 'bumping sound' that the Tower residents had heard, was caused by the potatoes as they fell from one step to another! Finally, after some concerted effort, the potatoes ended their journey in a wine cellar, where presumably they would be devoured by the rodent's family. [37]

ELLEN SHEARER

In the space of over four hundred years, many people have lived and no doubt a number have died at Turton Tower. Few, however, have troubled to write about the time they spent there. One lady named Ellen Rigg, whose name changed to Shearer, when she married, wrote a book about the time, when as a young girl, she lived at the Tower. She and her family were tenants there between the years 1895 and 1903.

The book reveals that Ellen and her three siblings were 'overjoyed' when they heard that there was a ghost at the Tower. They were told that the ghost was that of 'a white lady in a rustling silk dress, who wandered up and down the stairs.' In her book she muses that people were generally surprised when they were told that she and the children used to get out of their beds during the night and wait to see if the ghost might appear.

Ellen mentions that one night the family dogs were making a row and indicating that someone was present at the side door. As she hastily climbed out of bed she failed to see where she had put her dressing gown and chose instead to wrap herself in a 'white counterpane.' She ran quickly down the stairs and reached the side door which she managed to jar open. Standing in the doorway was a policeman who was taken aback by the ghostly sight and audibly gasped. "My, you did give me a fright. I thought you were the white lady!" [38]

In those days it was customary for a policeman to have an allocated area of the town, or 'beat' as it was usually called and for which he was responsible. One of his duties was to try the front door handles of certain properties and to make sure that they were locked.

Ellen recalls that on another occasion the policeman actually found the front door of the Tower to be unlocked. He tried to summon the attention of the household but was unable to get anyone to heed his call. After a little while he got the idea to sound a large gong, which he saw standing inside the entrance hall. This produced the desired effect and Ellen's father soon came running, whilst all the while thinking that the Tower was on fire. Everything turned out alright in the end but the writer wonders who had unlocked the front door? Could it have been the work of the white lady?

DOREEN HOUGH

Photo No 18 (circa: 2014)
Doreen (Left) with her sister Elsie (Right)

Doreen Hough (nee Pike) and her sister, Elsie, share the distinction of being the last members of the public to have lived at Turton Tower. As young girls, in 1948, they lived with their father who was named, Job and also with their aunt and uncle, Albert Barrett, who was the official caretaker. In 1962 Doreen was married and left the Tower but her family continued to live there until 1965. The writer was curious to know if any paranormal activity occurred during Doreen's life spent at the Tower. The following is what she had to say:

> "Often; knowing that I lived there for all that time; from 1948 to 1962 on getting married, everyone always says "did you ever see any ghosts?" I personally never saw a ghost and yet I came home at all hours in the night when I was in the police force but I still didn't see anything untoward; but I know that my dad did. I can remember my aunty telling me that one day he suddenly walked into the house and she was taken aback and exclaimed "good heavens Job have you seen a ghost?" and he said "Yes!" Then he explained what had happened. He said that he was sat at the front of the Tower, beneath

where the sundial is built into the stonework and was having a smoke; when suddenly he saw a woman dressed in a long black skirt. From within the base of the two yew trees, my father saw a lady, who was wearing a long black skirt. She came out from the trees and walked across the lawn. He instantly thought "who is this and what is she doing?" He stood up and walked diagonally across the lawn and down towards where she was walking. He was more or less near to her, near the trees by this time, as she had walked across the width of the lawn, when suddenly, he saw she had gone! It had obviously and definitely unnerved him because my aunty knew there was something wrong when he went into the house."

To clarify this part of the story, the reader may note that in front of the peel Tower, there is a lawn that stretches away towards the main public roadway. At the end of the lawn is a stone pillar. Situated between the pillar and the Tower are two large and mature yew trees that are set in line with each other. The trees are growing adjacent to and parallel with, a tarred driveway that links the front entrance of the Tower to the double steel gates at the end of the drive.

STORIES OF GHOSTLY DOGS AT TURTON TOWER
After Doreen had described her father's ghostly experience, she went on to disclose a few more incidents which revolved around the subject of dogs. Doreen remembered, "There was an elderly lady from the village, who was a friend of mine. She owned a pet spaniel and used to take the dog for a walk around the Tower. She said to me one day, "I'm not going back to the Tower; I shan't be going to the Tower again." Naturally I asked her why? She said, "Well when I was taking Sam (Doreen thinks that the dog was called Sam) around the back of the Tower, the dog stopped abruptly in his tracks and

refused to go any further." When the lady referred to 'the back of the Tower,' she meant that she and her dog were walking on a path that runs parallel to the railway line and towards a stone building that is presently known as 'the stables.' Doreen insists that her friend couldn't induce the dog to move forward and had a 'job' to get it to go back to the exit. "Now, when she returned the following day, for a daily walk," Doreen added, "the dog refused to get out of the car!" Doreen empathized with her friend and assured her that she had not heard of anything that might give rise to the dog's actions.

Of course that status quo was about to change as Doreen now relates. "So I was aware of this, when quite a while afterwards I was doing a talk." (Doreen gives talks to various organised groups upon request and during which she speaks about her life spent at the Tower.) "I had never mentioned the lady and Sam, the dog, but that same evening after the talk, a certain lady approached me and shared her story."

"Do you know my son has a Labrador" she said. "On one occasion when he took it for a walk in the Tower's grounds, the Labrador stopped dead and wouldn't move. My son said it wouldn't go forward or backwards and he had a great struggle to get it back to the car. He complained that he would never take the dog back to the Tower again!" After hearing this revelation, Doreen told the informant the story about her friend and Sam the dog.

Some weeks later, when Doreen gave another talk, she told both stories about the two different dog incidents. Perhaps thinking that she had exhausted the subject, she was suddenly surprised when a lady from the audience come forward and said to her, "I know somebody that had a dog that did exactly the same!" The lady didn't add any detail to her announcement and the subject appeared to be ended. However, Doreen informed the writer that some time later she did another talk at Turton Tower and saw a lady that she knew, who was sitting at the back of the audience.

During her talk Doreen spoke about the three incidents related to dogs. Some weeks later she happened to see the lady's daughter in the grounds of the Tower. Doreen explained, "She came to me and said, "My mother came to listen to your talk some time ago and you talked about some incidents involving dogs." I said, "Yes that's right, I remember" and then she said, "Well, you know, my mum had an experience with our dog!" I told the daughter that I'd seen her mother nudging her friend, as I was talking about the dog stories but I informed her that her mother hadn't come to speak with me."

The writer learned that Doreen had heard about the dog stories over a period of some ten to fifteen years prior to our talk. Following this revelation Doreen continued to recall that about the month of January 2013, when she visited the Tower's Victorian Tea Room, she was approached by some persons. "I had gone to the Tea Room at the Tower," said Doreen, "when the lady in charge of the Tea Room said to two men who were standing there, "this is the lady that you want to talk to." So I said, "why what's your problem?" One of the men said, "Apparently you lived here didn't you?" I said, "Well, yes" and I told him the time period. Then he asked, "Well did you ever see anything?" Meaning of course, did I see any ghosts, to which I replied, no I didn't, but my dad did."

The man asked me what happened and so I told him about the incident and started to describe the lady that my dad had seen. But before I could complete my story the man finished off my description. He told me what the lady was wearing and I said "Well you're right" then he said, "She's called Elizabeth and there's a big dog here too; it's either a Great Dane or an Irish wolfhound but it's quite big." So I said, "Well I'd never heard about the dog being here in the spirit and at the Tower."

"It would appear that the two men were either mediums or spiritualists, well; I think they call themselves 'ghost busters' really. After they had gone I was thinking about what they had told me and then I remembered that as a little girl I saw a kind of monument placed at the rear of the Tower. It was very grand but you could tell it was the grave of an animal. It was so grand that we thought it might have been for a horse but it could have been for a dog. [39]

It wasn't one that would be put there for an ordinary person's animal; it must have been put there by the Lord of the Manor. But it isn't there anymore and I don't know if it has fallen down but there is no sign of it at all. When I think about it, if that dog was at the Tower, he would be the guard dog and the only dog around. He would be the Lord of the Manor's dog. Furthermore, there wouldn't be all these paths where all the dogs walk nowadays. You know there are loads of dogs walking about the grounds these days and I'm convinced that it's the spirit of the 'big dog' that's scaring the little dogs away."

THE LADY IS CALLED 'ELIZABETH'

Doreen Hough's account of her father's sighting of the mysterious lady and the information given by the two male visitors to the Victorian Tea Room, prompted the writer to ask Doreen a few more questions.

Question: "Concerning the first incident when your father saw the apparition, what year would that be?"

Answer: "That would be in the 1950s. It would be shortly after the museum was formed. We hadn't been there very long; yes it would be the 1950s."

Question: "At that time had all the furniture arrived from all the various locations?"

Answer: "Yes, definitely, because the furniture started to arrive more or less when Mister Ashworth gave the Council a thousand pounds of his own money towards the foundation of a museum. It was also when Bradshaw Hall was being demolished. We were there in 1948. The furnishings and fine art that belonged to Colonel Hardcastle, of Bradshaw Hall, were either purchased or donated but they arrived at Turton Tower about 1950-52. That's more or less the time they were making the Tower into a museum. All the swords and all the guns and the horse brasses came from Bradshaw Hall. Lots of clocks came from Bradshaw Hall too. There was more clocks and furniture that came from Birtenshaw Hall when George Ashworth died."

Photo No 19 (circa: 1956)
The Sitting Room of Turton Tower

Photo No 19 portrays Turton Tower's visitors reception area. It looks as it did, when it was used as a sitting room by Doreen Hough and her family. The fire-place in its entirety was brought from Bradshaw Hall at the time of its demolition. Doreen remembers the fire-place arriving in singular stone blocks and each one numbered so that they could be re-assembled in conformity to a sketch.

Question: "Did your father describe the lady in any greater detail?"
Answer: "Not really, he just said she was wearing a long black skirt. We ladies of the early 1950s didn't wear long black skirts and it was just unusual. So he wondered what she was doing and walked across to her."
Question: "Did he experience anything else after that encounter?"

Answer: "No, but of course there is a cradle at the Tower that is supposed to rock by itself. I think my uncle once said he saw it rocking."

WRITER'S NOTE:

The 'rocking cradle' that Doreen mentions is the one that was brought from Bradshaw Hall to the Tower. Doreen also recalled that after sighting the 'ghostly lady' her father had no further unworldly experiences. However, there was one unforeseen event that was about to take place.

THE FIRE AT TURTON TOWER

During the month of July, in the year 1954, work began on restoring the second floor Bradshaw Room and the adjacent Ashworth Room. It was prompted by the discovery of defects in the lead gutters in that particular part of the building. This had resulted in causing excessive dampness to the room's decorations. Workmen opened up the flooring to check the extent of the damage and soon discovered that dry rot in the Bradshaw Room would require the replacement of one of the floor joists and the skirting boards near to the fireplace.

The Turton Tower Museum had been up and running for two years by the time the rooms were affected. They each contained a number of exhibits and not least were the mysterious Timberbottom Farm skulls. Because of the Tower's Museum status and in order to comply with the fire safety regulations, a number of portable fire extinguishers and fixed hose reels had to be installed throughout the building. It transpired, as subsequent events would show, it was just as well that they were.

On the morning of the 5th of January 1955, a strong, cold wind was blowing. Repairs to the Tower rooms, which called for the partial removal of the outside wall, had been underway for some days. The removal of the outside wall had exposed the bedrooms of both Doreen Hough and her sister, as well as the adjacent bedroom of their Aunt and Uncle.

It so happened that their bedrooms were directly below the Bradshaw Room and the Ashworth Room. In order to maintain the privacy of the tenants and to keep the wind from blowing through the building, tarpaulin sheeting was draped from the roof level and down to the ground. Additionally, a burning brazier was set in place close to the bedrooms, which served to keep the chill off the air.

Doreen recalls that she was not at college that day since the new term had not yet begun. Her sister Elsie, who was a year or two older, had already left the Tower to go to work. What happened next is only speculation but the fact is that the tarpaulin caught alight. Did a 'spark from the brazier' as the newspaper report suggested, trigger the tarpaulin to burn, or had the tarpaulin sheet blown against the brazier and caught fire? The exact cause was never established but whatever it might have been, within a few seconds the sheet was in flames.

Doreen's uncle, Albert Barrett, (55yrs of age) was the first to become aware of the fire and quickly roused the others. He was no stranger to drama since he was a veteran of the First World War and had once been wounded whilst serving with the Lancashire Fusiliers. It was soon discovered that the telephone line had been 'burnt through' and so communication with the emergency services was null and void. But Albert was a resourceful man and had the presence of mind to send his wife to the nearby farmhouse from where she was able to summons the Bolton Fire Brigade.

By this time the fire 'raged on scaffolding and tarpaulin' with such ferocity that it could be seen by the Station Master at Turton Railway Station; which stood two or three hundred yards away. Remembering the recently installed fire hoses, Albert quickly put the one nearest to the blaze into action. He instructed Doreen to assist him by feeding off the hose pipe from its reel, whilst he dragged it towards the fire.

Photo No 20 (circa: 1950s)
Albert Barrett holds a gift from some
Canadian people who visited the Tower

The temporary asphalted roof was burning fiercely by this time and was described as being 'spectacular' while it lasted. The flames were rapidly licking their way towards the roof but Albert 'tackled the outbreak from below the ceiling and held it in check until the fire brigade arrived.' [40] He played water onto the flames and thus prevented them from spreading into the main Tower building. Thankfully the Fire Brigade Station was only four miles away and so the fire fighters were quickly on the scene. Fortunately, by the time they arrived Albert had the fire under control.

The Fire Chief Officer, Mister R. Bentley, stated that in his opinion the fire could have had 'serious consequences on a historic monument like Turton Tower,' had it not been for the prompt action of Mr. Barrett. These comments were later endorsed at a meeting of Turton Council, when Albert was congratulated on his 'promptitude and presence of mind.' [41] The fire damage was largely confined to beams and joists but the Bradshaw Room, which was directly above where Doreen and her sister had their bedroom, together with the adjacent Ashworth Room, had to be completely refurbished.

Visitors of today will see that the walls of the two rooms are smooth and square and that the floor is quite level. This is all a consequence of the restoration work carried out following the fire. Above the smooth surface of the ceiling and out of public sight, are the original charred beams that still remain as a silent testimony to the event.

Photo No 21 (circa: 1955)
Inspecting the bedrooms after the fire

Photograph No 21 was taken on the day after the fire. A man is pictured looking into the burnt-out bedrooms. In the lower left hand corner of the photo can be seen the top portion of the two sisters' bedroom. On closer inspection, wall paper can be seen to cover the wall. Immediately above this is a steel joist that stretches from left to right across the photo. Above the joist on the left hand side of the photo can be seen the Bradshaw Room. Next to it, on the right of the photo and more or less in line with the head of the posing figure, is the Ashworth Room. The suspected cause of the fire was that the tarpaulin may have blown onto a burning brazier or that a spark from the same may have caused an ignition. But could this be an example of the work of a poltergeist?

THE GHOST AT THE BUS STOP

Photo No 22 (circa: 2015)
Turton Tower Bus Stop

One stormy Saturday night, in February of 1954, a single-deck bus was travelling the route from Bromley Cross towards the White Horse public house at Edgworth. The driver was Mr. Frank Edwards, a stockily built 34 year old, who lived at Lee Street in Bolton. With its head lights turned on, the bus travelled slowly through the falling rain and made its way up the hill towards Turton Tower. Frank was wearing his regulation military styled uniform, complete with peaked cap and was keeping a watchful eye open for would-be passengers.

As Frank's bus drew closer to the Turton Tower bus stop he caught sight of what looked to be an elderly gentleman, who was standing there. Frank had enough time to observe the man whom he described as wearing a 'light raincoat, grey trousers, brown shoes, a white cap and he was carrying a white stick'. [42] As the bus was pulling into the kerb the old man stepped forward in apparent readiness to step on board and then he 'waited.' Frank's experienced hands brought the bus to a halt with its entrance doors directly in-line with the waiting gentleman.

Speaking 'bluntly,' as Frank was inclined to do, he said, "I looked at him through the door-window, pressed the 'Open' button and as the doors slowly moved apart; he disappeared!" By gesturing with a wave of his arm, Frank emphasised his statement and then added, "I felt the hair standing up on my neck."

The scare in itself was bad enough but Frank was puzzled by something he saw. He said, "The funny thing was, that although it was raining heavily, this fellow was perfectly dry." Frank added, "I didn't think anything of it at the time, but I've done some thinking lately." The experience undoubtedly shook Frank as it was something that was completely new to him; after all is said and done, it's not every day that one sees a person disappear and as the stage magician might say; 'before your very eyes!'

Naturally Frank would want to share his experience with people and that is just what he did. His wife was first to hear of his encounter and she later admitted, "I didn't believe him when he came home." Of course his work mates at the Bullock Street bus depot, where Frank was based, learned of his experience and their reaction was to taunt Frank unmercifully; which is what might be expected. But Frank brushed off their jibes saying, "Let them laugh. It frightened me to death, I don't mind admitting. Wouldn't surprise me if some of the other drivers have seen this chap and they won't speak up."

For Frank it could be that the apparition may have been a one off because as he says, "I've passed the same spot hundreds of times, before and since, but without seeing the spook." When asked what Frank might do, should he happen to see the gentleman again, he replied, "If I see him again I think I'll get out of the bus and see what goes on. It's given me a shock, I don't mind saying but I don't suppose it can do any harm. He looked a wizened little chap, quite friendly." [43]

Frank Edwards was exceptionally observant to see that the gentleman was actually wearing 'brown shoes'! His description of the man, saying that he was 'quite friendly,' could only have been based upon a visual appraisal. After all there is no mention of any dialogue having been exchanged between them. For Frank to observe what the man was wearing is plausible. Considering it could have been no more than six feet from where he was standing to where Frank was sitting in the driver's seat,

It may be noted that this report predates a similar one made by Doris Walker, who lived at the Tower during the 1970s. She mentioned that 'an old lady' was seen at the same bus stop and when the bus stopped for her to board, she 'disappeared'. Sadly the writer cannot find any reference to the 'old lady' and wonders if the account that was given by Frank has morphed over a span of twenty years into the one told by Doris. Or alternatively could the 'old lady' be the wife of the 'old man'?

GHOSTLY YOUNG COUPLE SEEN AT BUS STOP

There is yet another story relating to the Turton Tower bus stop, which occurred during the late 1970s. This story is taken from an internet website which purports to show the contents of a letter that was sent to the Bolton Evening News. The writer has made attempts to verify its authenticity but without success. However, in view of the way the story is presented the writer decided to include it in this narrative.

According to the article, one evening in November of 1978, a certain Mr Berry of Tonge Moor, near Bolton, decided to visit some friends who lived at Edgworth. It would seem that he travelled on a bus towards Turton Tower in a similar manner to Mr Frank Edwards, who was mentioned earlier.

The difference this time was that Mr Berry found himself to be occupying the bus with one other passenger, who happened to be an elderly lady. As the bus approached the stop Mr Berry rose from his seat in readiness to get off. He happened to notice a young couple standing at the bus stop who was bathed in the light from a street lamp. In a letter he subsequently wrote to the Bolton Evening News, he described the couple as being a girl of 'about 19 years old, with a wistful expression on her face and wearing a fawn raincoat.' The girl's companion was 'a bit older, with dark hair and wearing an anorak.'

As the bus pulled into the stop Mr Berry noticed that the elderly lady also wanted to get off and so he instinctively turned around to help her. Afterwards he was most surprised to find that the young couple were nowhere to be seen. He asked the lady if she had seen the pair and she confirmed that she had. She declared that she too was puzzled as to where they had gone. Mr Berry was sufficiently intrigued by the disappearance that he spent a 'few minutes' looking for the young people; no doubt under the patient and watchful eye of the bus driver. Since the brief search produced no positive result the bus continued its journey.

A couple of hours later, after Mr Berry had visited his friends, he made his return journey. He was surprised to find himself on a bus that was driven by the same driver, with whom he had travelled earlier that evening. Naturally the two men discussed the event. The driver readily recalled seeing the couple standing at the bus-stop but as he said, "They certainly weren't there when I stopped." According to the report, one or two other drivers have commented on the vanishing of the would-be passengers, who are seen to be waiting at the stop. [44]

MR & MRS SAM WEATHERALL
(1965-1968)

Photo No 23 (circa: 1966)
Mr Sam Weatherall with Jingles

In June of 1966, Sam Weatherall and his wife Jean, together with Moira, their 15-years old daughter and not forgetting Jingles, their pet dog, all lived at Turton Tower. They had lived there for just under two years and Sam's position was that of caretaker, or as the press sometimes say, 'custodian'. One of his many duties was to conduct the members of the Turton Council, through the Tower and to the Council Chamber, which is where they held their meetings. His other duties included the mammoth task of cleaning the mullioned windows, the oak panels and the carved furniture. There was also the hoovering of the carpets, the sweeping of the floors and the cutting of the grass on the lawns. All of this was done in his stride and it was said that he and his family collectively gave the Tower its 'undeniably warm and lived in atmosphere'.

As a matter of fact, one day, as Sam Weatherall was showing a party of visitors around the Tower, which was another one of his duties, his wife just happened to be in the kitchen, making apple and blackberry jam. The attendant smell of the cooking had permeated throughout the lower rooms whereupon, a lady, who was one of the visitors, 'sniffed appreciatively' and then announced "this is a marvellous old house. It actually smells lived-in." [45]

THE GHOST WHO ROCKS THE CRADLE

When asked about the subject of ghosts, Sam mentioned that a wooden cradle, along with other items of furniture, had been transported from Bradshaw Hall. He said he was aware, that there was mention of the ghost of a woman, who was said to rock the cradle at midnight but Sam added that in his opinion, the Tower had been owned by "too many good and happy men" for it to be haunted. However, he did acknowledge that if there *were* any ghosts at the Tower, then they must have been transplanted from other places! His daughter Moira would appear to have agreed with her father's sentiments because she was known to walk happily through the house alone and even at midnight. Similarly she didn't mind walking up the long tree-lined drive at night time, both in the dark and with the wind often blowing 'eerily' through the trees. [46]

WRITER'S NOTE:

The wooden cradle from Bradshaw Hall, is shown in Photo No 24. The year 1630, can be seen to have been carved into the end that faces the camera. There is also a portion of wood, missing from an upright column. It looks as if it has been cleanly sliced off and possibly by a bladed object. It may be noted that the Tower guides sometimes use the cradle as a prop, in the telling of its eerie history. During the explanation of its ghostly past, the cradle will start to slowly rock and seemingly by itself, thus causing the visitor some concern.

Photo No 24 (circa: 2014)
The rocking cradle at Turton Tower

Of course this is just a bit of show business on the part of the guide who quickly lets the visitor into the secret. In reality the cradle has been surreptitiously placed onto a stone slab, that is unevenly seated on the floor. When the slab is depressed at a specific point and in this case by the controlled foot of the guide; the cradle begins to rock!

THE CLOCK THAT STOPS AFTER MIDNIGHT

Although the Weatheralls had never actually seen a ghost or experienced anything unworldly, during their time at the Tower, there was one thing that Sam Weatherall admits he just couldn't explain. Yet another of Sam's duties was to wind-up the old long-case clocks that added to the visual décor of the Tower. He recalls that one particular clock that stood on the 'first landing,' regularly stopped functioning at 'exactly' thirty-five minutes after mid-night. During the daytime the clock ran fine but when the noted time came around; it simply stopped. He tried winding it up at different times and even just before going to bed. He hoped that the clock would keep ticking but it has always stopped at the same time.

WRITER'S NOTE:
The writer is aware that there are currently five long-case clocks within the Tower buildings. Since they were most probably moved to different locations throughout the years, it is not possible to say which clock is the one to which Sam Weatherall refers. Unfortunately, because of current procedures, none of them are kept wound-up. Wouldn't it make for an interesting experiment, if one day, they were put into motion again. Then, to see if one of them stops at the special time?

ALBERT AND DORIS WALKER
(1972-1975)

Doris Walker (57yrs of age) and her husband Albert (60yrs of age) had been caretakers of Turton Tower for just over three years when one day, during December of 1975, an elderly man hurried into their kitchen. Doris recalled, "He was so upset I had to make him a cup of tea." The man explained that he had been walking in 'Chetham Close,' when he saw a lady with a dog on a leash that was walking towards him. As they drew closer to him he noticed that the lady was wearing an 'old fashioned hat' and 'a long coat down to her ankles' and as the old saying goes, they passed like ships in the night.

The man courteously raised his hat and said, "Good morning" but there was no reply from the lady and no sound from the dog; in fact they both seemed to 'drift silently' passed him. Suddenly, he thought that the lady's appearance was a little strange, so he turned around to take a second look but as he did so he found that both she and her dog had 'completely disappeared.' The man hastened his journey and having arrived at the Tower told Mrs Walker what had happened to him. [47]

GHOSTLY COACH AND HORSES

It wasn't the first time that Doris Walker had heard stories of paranormal activities that had happened in the neighbourhood. There was one that was witnessed by several people, who were said to have seen a stage coach and horses, which were driven over the moor, in the direction once taken by an old Roman road. Apparently the stage coach is said to have driven through what is now a private house but used to be an old barn and shippon that belonged to Turton Tower, in the days when it was an estate.

HAUNTED BUS STOP

Doris Walker also recalled that there have been reports that 'an old lady' stands at the bus stop, which is situated near to the main entrance to the Tower and when the bus draws in to pick her up, she disappears!

THE ASHWORTH ROOM AT TURTON TOWER

Cleaning the various rooms of the Tower was one of the jobs that Doris Walker undertook but the Ashworth Room was one she particularly didn't like working in. She confessed that it had a 'horrible feel' for her and she admitted that she was always 'glad to get out of it'. It seems she wasn't alone with her opinion of the room because as she recalled, the 'many visitors' to the room had stated that they too didn't like the atmosphere.

LIVING AND WORKING AT THE TOWER

As already mentioned the Walker couple had worked at the Tower for just over three years and were generally quite happy but Doris remembered what happened when she and her husband first arrived there. She found that she couldn't sleep much at night because of the various noises that they experienced. There were 'creaking and banging sounds' and 'thuds and groans' but they thought that the sounds were due to the Tower being old and having a lot of wood internally. Presumably the wood could possibly give rise to the unwanted sounds by expanding and contracting as the ambient temperatures changed. Doris did however, confirm that as time went on, she was eventually able to sleep, since she had grown accustomed to the sounds.

INEXPLICABLE EXPERIENCE ON THE STAIRCASE

During the period that the Walkers lived at the Tower, Doris recounted that she had experienced something that *was* inexplicable. It happened a few times when she had been cleaning on the last flight of stairs before the Chetham Room. It seems that as she was working she felt a 'crinoline dress brush against her legs.' She got the notion that a ghostly lady was there who wanted to keep an eye on something in the Chetham Room and so she watches who goes near.

HAUNTING THE VISITORS

It so happened that amidst the stories of fear and wonder, there was a lighter moment in the tenancy of the Walkers, as Doris laughingly recalls. She explained that in the early hours of one summer morning before dawn had broke, a party of revellers drove up to the Tower in a motor-car and the occupants jumped out. In their inebriated state they began frolicking about the lawn and during their antics caused sufficient noise to wake the Walkers from sleep. Doris was the first to jump out of bed and head for a window, from where she could see the uninvited visitors.

Her mind was working in top gear at that moment for she decided to have some fun of her own. She opened the window wide enough, so that the unwelcome intruders could clearly see her, as she gazed out. She must have presented a frightening spectacle, as it was certainly no fair Juliet that looked out from the window! With her long white hair hanging loose about her shoulders and wearing a long white nightdress, Doris called out loudly in a pretend ghostly voice, "What do you want?" The startled gathering wasted no time in answering, as they scrambled into their motor-car in a state of abject panic and sped away! [48]

THE SPECTRE OF TURTON TOWER

Living in the village of Chapeltown, near Turton, is Mrs. Barbara Fisher, who remembers that in December of 1985, she attended an event at Turton Tower. As a result of much discussion that was had in previous months, flood lights had been installed to illuminate the outside of the buildings. By way of celebrating this modern convenience, a gathering of people was arranged to meet at the Tower, at which refreshments would be provided. As the evening was winding down, Barbara Fisher and her then husband, made their way to the parking area to find their car, with a view to travelling home.

At the time of the event and contrary to today's rules, parking was allowed close to the Tower buildings. It was also acceptable to park along the driveway, that extends from the property and away towards the double-steel entrance gates. That evening Barbara had taken a camera along with her, with the thought of maybe clicking a couple of snaps of her friends. The camera was nothing special and today she is not sure if it had a built-in flash but it *was* loaded with a roll of 35mm colour film.

As a parting thought she chose to take a couple of pictures of the illuminated building, although she half expected them not to be successful. Four of the photographs that were created that night have survived and are numbered Photo No 25, Photo No 26, Photo No 27 and Photo No 28. Two of the group (Photos 25 and 26) were taken near the entrance area and pictured in them can be seen a few motor cars that are parked close by. The third and fourth photos (Photos No 27 and 28) as it happened turned out to be of particular interest. If the reader is an experienced photographer then please don't be alarmed by the look of the buildings, since the verticals appear to converge due to the limitations of the camera.

It will be remembered that Barbara Fisher couldn't recall if her camera had a built in flash. However, in Photo No 26 it can be observed that the number plates of both parked cars appear to be reflecting light.

Photo No 25 (circa: 1985)
Entrance area to Turton Tower

This may well be caused by an integral flash belonging to the camera. There is also a strong shadow to the left of the red car which suggests that a floodlight is shining from the right hand side of the scene but is not captured in the picture. Indeed the building itself is well lit and must surely have been illuminated by a floodlight and not solely by a camera flash.

After taking Photos No 25 and No 26, Barbara and her husband turned around and walked along the driveway that leads away from the buildings. Within the space of a few strides the couple stopped and turned once more to face the buildings with the camera. Two more snaps were taken within seconds of each other and Photos No 27 and No 28 are the result.

The Photo No 27 captures a row of cars parked on the left, that begin at the buildings and extend towards the photographer, with one of them being closest to the camera. They stand on the edge of a driveway that lies both in front of and behind the camera.

Photo No 26 (circa: 1985)
Entrance area to Turton Tower

It may be noted that the cars that are parked against the far buildings are visible in all four photographs and light appears to be reflected from their number plates. Again, this would suggest that a flash from the camera had been used in an attempt to illuminate the subject. At the time of taking the photographs, Barbara and her husband were not aware of the white 'form,' that is clearly visible in Photos No 27 and No 28. It is only when the film was processed and the photographs obtained that the phenomena was seen.

Photo No 27 (circa: 1985)
A ghostly form-

Photo No 28 (circa: 1985)
A ghostly form-

At this point in the report the reader may well be asking the question "What is the 'form' that is present in Photos No 27 and 28?" An impartial answer would surely have to be: whatever it is, it certainly gives rise to a number of debateable questions and some of which are listed below.

[Question] Could it be the leaves of a tree-branch blowing in front of the camera lens?

[Answer] Barbara is adamant that she was fully aware of anything that may have been obstructing the camera lens and that was definitely not the case.

[Question] Did the camera flash play a role in 'creating' the 'form?'

[Answer] A study of photos No 27 and No 28 strongly suggest that the camera was fitted with a flash gun and that it fired when the exposures were made. In both photographs it can be seen that the number plates of the parked cars are reflecting the flash light. It may also be noted that the cars nearest to the camera are illuminated. This condition can only be brought about by the camera flash, since the floodlights are positioned near to the building and out of reach of the cars.

In photo No 28 the form appears to be transparent in its upper portion but solid in its lower part. Also the flash appears to have penetrated the upper portion but not the lower. Having considered the evidence, the writer finds it difficult to imagine how the flash could have 'created' the 'form.'

[Question] Could it have been exhaust smoke from an automobile?

[Answer] Again Barbara insists that no automobile had its engine running at the time that the photographs were taken.

[Question] Exhaust smoke has been mentioned but what about cigarette smoke? Is it possible that there might have been cigarette smoke present?

[Answer] Neither Barbara or her husband was aware of the ghostly 'form,' until they saw the photos that they had obtained from the processing shop.

Barbara admitted that her husband was a cigarette smoker but both were agreed that the 'form' had not been caused by cigarette smoke.

[Question] What about a defect in the processing of the film?

[Answer] That question is more difficult to answer and needs more consideration. No one can say emphatically that a fault did not occur in the processing of the film. But if that was the case then why would it be, that in just two frames of a whole roll of film, there should be the 'white forms'? Bearing in mind that the roll of film would have consisted of some twenty-four or thirty-six frames?

[Question] What happened to the negatives of the roll of film?

[Answer] Barbara explains that at the time the photographs were taken, there was naturally some interest in the result of the four photos in question. But considering them not to be of any great value or interest to other parties, they ended up in a drawer in the way photographs normally do. Then, with the passage of time and we are now looking at almost 30 years since the photos were taken, the negatives and corresponding photos from the same roll of film, have long since been lost. It was probably because of the event and the special nature of Photos No 27 and No 28 that they survived.

[Question:] Just what then is the 'form'?

[Answer:] It looks like it could be mist or smoke and it also looks as though it could be a shape of someone. The part of the 'form,' as seen in the left upper quarter of Photo No 28, appears to be the rough shape of a woman's head. It seems to be averted towards its right hand side or, possibly, it is looking straight at the camera. If the viewer looks lower down, there appears to be a pair of 'shoulders' and then with a little more concentration, there appear to be 'two arms' that are protruding outwards from the 'shoulders' and towards the camera. The arms curve inwards and look as though they have two clenched fists that are gently touching each other at the knuckles.

The 'arms' are more dense in appearance than the other parts of the body.

The shape of the 'form' in Photos No 27 and No 28 are quite different to one another and yet the scene in the background remains the same. The automobiles are still parked in the same position and the photographer has positioned the camera with minimal difference, from one exposure to the next. This observation gives rise to the suggestion that the two exposures were taken within a short time span of each other.

The writer observes that the 'form' in Photo No 28 appears to be partially made up of a series of circles. When viewed closely the circles appear to be individually placed but when viewed from a distance they appear to merge. If this observation is true then the circles could have some connection with the so called 'orbs' that are often seen when using digital photography. The concept of 'orbs' will be dealt with in more depth later in this book.

In the final analysis of these incredible photographs, the writer expresses the view that considering the reported activity throughout the years, both within and around Turton Tower it seems highly likely that the photographs are genuine. Conversely, it is highly unlikely that there has been an accident with the processing of the film. Of course cigarette smoke is perhaps the prime suspect for the cause but Barbara Fisher maintains that no one was smoking at the time and therefore her statement has to be respected. The writer suggests that the 'form' could be a spirit who possibly wanted to be noticed and maybe wanted to make contact. By manifesting itself in this manner, was a way of attempting to do that and perhaps the only way possible. The final consideration in this whole incident is to ponder whether the 'form' *is* an entity and if so does it have a consciousness?

THE MAN WEARING A TOP HAT

Mr. Ken Holden is a retired farmer and lives in the village of Chapeltown, near Turton. One year during the 1990s and around the month of August, he received a 'phone call to say that one of his cows was calving. It so happened that the land on the opposite side of the road to the main entrance to Turton Tower, was owned by the farmer and it was there that his cattle grazed. He and his uncle, along with a friend called Graham Johnson, drove in their Land Rover from Chapeltown to the farmer's field; with a view to tending to the needs of the expectant bovine.

On arrival Ken drove the Land Rover in an outward arc and then swung it back again, so as to bring it in line with the entrance gate to the field. Road traffic in those days wasn't as busy as it is today, so they had enough time to make the manoeuvre without the fear of causing an obstruction. As the Land Rover waited astride the road, with its front end facing the gate, the three occupants suddenly saw the figure of a man, who was standing on the road ahead of them and in line with the middle of the gateway. Ken Holden takes up the story:

> "The man just stood there. He was wearing a black top hat, with tails hanging from it and a long black Victorian styled coat; looking like an old time undertaker. His face was 'white' and he just stood there facing forward and staring, and not moving. My uncle got out of the vehicle and went across to open the gate. The man just stood there staring forward and not moving; even when my uncle walked passed him to open the gate, and the same again, when he came back to the vehicle. As my uncle climbed into the Land Rover he said, "I don't like the looks of him.""

As we drove towards the man he kept on staring forward and then he just moved to one side and we drove passed. When we had finished our job and came back to the gate to leave, we found that the man had gone. This happened at the weekend, probably on a Friday or Saturday night; but on the following Tuesday, I went into the 'Railway,' which is a public house located at Bromley Cross.

My dad and his friends used to play dominoes there every Tuesday night and as I walked in, Fred, who was one of my dad's mates, said, "Hey, did you see that fella that your dad said?" (Ken had obviously mentioned the incident to his father who in turn had told his 'mates' at the public house.)

I answered, "Yes." Fred then added, "Well, when I was coming from Bromley Cross, he was stood right under the middle of the railway bridge next to the King William's public house."

At this point Ken added that he thought Fred had been to see his father who was ill. Fred continued to tell Ken his story.

"I put my brakes on to slow down and he just stepped out of the way of my car, just like that; he frightened me to death." Ken was quick to add, "and that was the same night and roughly about the same time, that we saw the man but we've never heard or seen anything about him since that day." [49]

Ken Holden's statement prompted the writer to ask the following questions:

[Question] "Was there anywhere the man could have hidden when you went into the field?"
[Answer] "Well, when we went into the field the man could have gone anywhere, I suppose. Because when we came out of the field he was nowhere to be seen. The bridge next to the King William public house is just down the dip from Turton Tower, on the road leading to Bromley Cross and of course the 'Railway' public house. The two separate sightings were more or less the same time; so I suppose the man could have gone down to the bridge, having left the field.

[Question] "Well would you say the man was a 'spook' or what?"
[Answer] "I don't know what the hell it was; it was funny; (strange) It made the hair on the back of your neck stand up; there was something just not right."

At this point in the interview Ken's wife added the following comment; "They both came back and they said to me, "We've just had a strange experience." Then she turned towards her husband saying, "and it shook you all up didn't it?"
Ken agreed wholeheartedly and said, "Yes, and I've never seen anything like it, either before or since!"

WRITER'S NOTE:
The farmer's field that is mentioned in the above incident, is located on the opposite side of the road, to the 'haunted' Turton Tower bus-stop. The same bus-stop that is described in an earlier chapter!

LIZZIE JONES

In December of 2011 the writer attended a function at Turton Tower, where a monologue was presented by the actress and writer, Lizzie Jones. Having an avid interest in medieval history and a flair for acting, she presented her interpretation of an event, in the life of Mary Queen of Scots. Her performance highlighted lesser known facets about the nature of the ill-fated Queen. Due to the size of the room, she was brought to close quarters with her audience, which caused her to display her faultless talent. Since she wished to look the part, she went to the trouble of making her own dress and trimmings, which matched the likeness of one that had been worn by the Queen herself.

Collectively, Mary Queen of Scots was imprisoned for almost nineteen years but Lizzie Jones chose a period in the year 1569, when the Queen was imprisoned at the cold and unpleasant Tutbury Castle, near Derby. Her presentation was flawless and remembering over an hour of dialogue was a stretch of anyone's memory. After the performance I asked if I might take a photograph of her and she readily agreed. Like most good photographers I took a number of photos in the hope of getting the 'perfect one.' I took three of her standing upright, which of course would show her dress to the best advantage. Afterwards, whilst wishing to add a little variety, I took two additional photos as she was seated next to a table.

The venue was restrictive for taking the photographs, since people were still seated to the left of the camera and the only available space was that nearest to a doorway. Behind the subject can be seen a portion of the original cruck-frame timbers. They support the roof of one section of the Tower complex. I was mindful of people starting to move around and I feared that someone might walk in front of the camera. That fear however, turned out to be unwarranted and my photo shoot progressed without impediment.

All five photographs were taken within seconds of each other. This fact is verified by my camera, which has the facility to automatically record the time and date when the exposure was made. After subsequently looking at photos No 29, 30 and 31, I noticed that the time of 21:57hrs. is recorded on each of the exposures. The time shown is the same for each exposure and thus confirms that they were taken literally within seconds of each other.

Photo No 29 [Taken on 10/12/2011 @ 21:57hrs.]

No sooner had I shot Photo No 29 when I realised that the lower edge of the dress was cropped. To remedy this, I moved back a couple of paces in order to fully frame the subject. At the same time I tried to ignore a portion of a chair, which is seen to be intruding on the bottom left-corner of the scene. Naturally I tried to move the offending article but found it to be attached to a whole row.

Photo No 30-[Taken on 10/12/2011 @21:57hrs.]

Photo No 31-[Taken on 10/12/2011 @ 21:57hrs.]

The second photo in the series was Photo No 30, which managed to frame the whole subject but was still not acceptable. I asked the subject to turn her face towards the camera and then I tried again. The resultant image in Photo No 31 was finally agreeable. Having decided to change the pose of the 'Queen' I asked if I might take two more shots of her in a seated position and whilst holding a pewter goblet. A table and goblet, together with an old candle and candlestick, were props that were used during her earlier performance.

If the reader looks carefully at the Queen's dress, there is a small piece of white material, strand-like in shape, which appears to be clinging to the fabric. It is present in all three photographs and can be seen at the front centre of the subject and just about knee height. However, Photo No 31 has something extra that appears in the upper part of the dress. The additional extra is known as an 'orb' and can be seen at the level of the 'Queen's' waist-line and on her left side.

The following photographs, which are Photos No 31A and Photo No 31B are enlargements of Photo No 31 and show the 'orb' in greater detail.

Photo No 31A

A careful study of Photo No 31B will reveal a much smaller orb that can be seen in the bottom right-hand corner. The two together conjure a thought that the larger one is a planet and the smaller one is its moon. Or could they be two spirits; one tall and the other short and possibly of children?

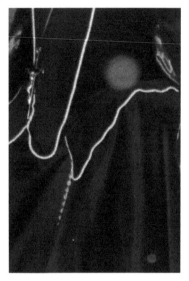

Photo No 31B

WHAT ARE ORBS?

The reader who is not familiar with the word 'orb' may well be wondering and asking the mental question, what are orbs? The answer is that orbs are something that has come into prominence mainly since the introduction of digital cameras. That is not to say that they were unheard of before digital cameras were invented but they are certainly more widely known now, than before. At the time of photographing a subject, orbs are usually invisible to the naked eye but are quite visible on the resulting camera image.

They can appear in various shapes but usually take the form of translucent circles, having a translucent pattern in their inner part, which looks rather like the pattern of a snowflake. Sometimes the orbs can take the form of a solid circular blob and are coloured yellow and look very much like the yoke of an egg. At other times they can appear in the shape of small sausage-like streaks of solid light. It is thought by paranormal investigators that orbs are energy forms which constitute a departed person's intelligence, or at least their motive force.

Sceptics on the other hand, maintain that orbs are simply specks of dust, which are caught on camera as they float in the air. The dust is said to float between the camera lens and the subject that is being photographed and that the flash-light reflects off the dust particle, thus creating an image. It is also thought that orbs are caused by dust or dirt, which is actually present on the camera lens. Of course any photographer worthy of their salt would normally make sure that the camera lens is kept clean.

Photo No 32-[Taken on 10/12/2011] @ 21:59hrs.]

Please note that no orbs are visible in Photos No 32 and 33 and yet they were taken within a minute or two of Photo No 31. Similarly there are no orbs present in Photos No 29 and 30. If dust is expected to be present for any photograph then surely it should have been present for Photos No 32 and 33 since the movement of the writer, the subject and

Photo No 33-[Taken on 10/12/2011@ 21:59hrs.]

especially the movement of the table and chair, would have caused maximum disturbance of the floor area and thus produce maximum airborne dust.

But in all honesty, the writer finds it very hard to believe that a speck of dust, could cause an image to appear that is the size of that which is visible in Photo No 31. In closing this subject, it may be of interest for the reader to know, that the writer has taken photographs in various rooms of Turton Tower and on different occasions. Of the rooms in which paranormal activity has been reported, the writer's camera has 'captured' images of orbs.

MIRIAM DISLEY

Miriam Disley lives at Breightmet, near Bolton and was an employee at Turton Tower between the years 1991-1995. Following a short break, she worked again at the Tower from 2001-2010, after which time she retired. One of her duties at the Tower was to enter the various rooms at closing time and prepare them for the evening.

This meant first closing the blinds that covered the windows and then drawing the curtains across the blinds. Additionally, any lights that might be switched on, she would turn them off. Conversely, when the Tower was opening for visitors at the beginning of the day, she would perform the same duties in the reverse order.

During the time that she had worked at the Tower, Miriam claims to have seen two ghostly figures. With curiosity raising its head the writer posed the following leading question:

[Question] What can you tell me about what you 'saw' at the Tower?

[Answer] "I never believed in ghosts before I worked at the Tower. I only believed in what I could see; which we shouldn't really, because I believe in the Lord (Jesus) and I know He's there and I know He's with me and I can't see Him. But I never believed in ghosts. My father once told me he had seen a ghost and I *did* believe him. But when I worked at the Tower some of the people who paid a visit used to ask me, "Have you seen any ghosts?" I used to say "No" and then they might say, "Well I've seen ghosts," meaning of course elsewhere. I used to think, "Yeah, all right," in my sceptical way".

THE GHOST IN THE BRADSHAW ROOM

"A couple of years before I retired from the Tower, (2008) I saw two different ghosts and each within weeks of one another. Both occasions happened to be on Bank Holidays and I think that the first one was either Good Friday or Easter Monday. It was about ten minutes before we opened to the public, which was at 12 noon. The caretaker had unlocked the doors and I was rushing around going from room to room, opening the curtains and making ready for the day's visitors. Then I got to the -. Now, I didn't like that Bradshaw Bedroom for some reason. What I used to do was to go into the dressing room first and turn the light on. Then I would come out and then go into the main bedroom and turn the light on in there.

I didn't like walking through the connecting doorway from the dressing room to the main Bradshaw Bedroom. (Miriam paused to think for a moment and then continued) No; I didn't like turning the light on in the dressing room and walking through."

[Question] What was it that made you not like going through from one room to the other?

[Answer] "I don't know; it's a feeling that I had from when I first started working there. But this particular day I had started at the top of the building, going from room to room and was making my way to the Bradshaw Bedroom. When I got to the dressing room I went in and switched the light on and then *walked through the connecting doorway*. It was something I didn't normally do. I got to the big window inside the bedroom and I drew the curtains back and when I turned around, there was a lady stood at the side of me. *I have never been as frightened in my life!*

The colour must have just drained out of me and I was out of that room and I have never moved as fast. I didn't want to go back in that room for a long time afterwards; it took a long time before I felt comfortable going in that room at all. My boss (Dennis Neale) saw me after I came out and asked me if I was alright. I told him I'd just seen a ghost. He said, "Have you really? Well you do look pale." I could not get used to the fact and still can't, that a ghost can look just like we look."

[Question] How did she look?

[Answer] "She wore a cloak. I didn't see her face. The feeling was horrible!"

[Question] Was she not looking at you?

[Answer] "I don't know; I just turned around and saw the cloak and bonnet".

[Question] Was she wearing a hooded cape?

[Answer] "Yes".

[Question] Was she wearing a dress?

[Answer] "I couldn't tell you. I didn't wait long enough. I was out! I never moved as fast".

[Question] So how did you know it was a woman?

[Answer] "Because she had a cloak on and I just took it that she was a woman".

[Question] Could it have been a monk?

[Answer] "It could have been a monk or a priest I don't know".

[Question] What made you think it was a woman?

[Answer] "I don't know it was just a feeling. But it wasn't a nice feeling!"

[Question] But you didn't see her face?

[Answer] "No".

[Question] What colour was the clothing?

[Answer] "It was dark; very dark. I would say more black than anything. Oh, it was scary!"

[Question] But you didn't see any features?

[Answer] "No, I didn't wait long enough. I mean the shock of me opening the curtains and turning around to see someone standing there that was taller than me (Miriam is about 5ft 5ins tall) that was it, I was off. *But it was an experience I would not wish to have missed.* Because it does tell me now that there is something else; there are spirits wandering somewhere. Also you could walk passed a ghost and not know that they *were* a ghost. That's the thing that gets me. Because they are just like we are".

THE GHOST IN THE MORNING ROOM

Miriam saw the second ghost within two weeks of seeing the first and thinks it might have been on the following Bank Holiday, which happened to be 'May Day.' On this occasion the Tower was being closed at the end of the day, which was about ten minutes to four o' clock in the afternoon. Miriam had been closing the blinds and curtains of the rooms in the upper levels and had now reached the ground level. She walked into the Morning Room, or Library, as it is sometimes called; evidenced by the fact that the room has wall to wall book-cases, that are filled with books.

Originally around the year 1500, the room had been a building of the cruck design with a thatched roof and had stood separate from the Tower. It wasn't until the middle 1800's that the Kay family joined everything together. They introduced the present wall panelling from Middleton Hall, near Manchester. The Hall was being demolished around that time.

Upon entering the room, Miriam saw the form of a man who was standing in front of the window. The sight of him caused her to stop abruptly in the doorway. He had his back to her and was apparently looking out of the window towards the lawn. There was a Pugin table between the man and Miriam so she couldn't see the lower part of his body, which included his legs and feet.

"His costume was absolutely wonderful, it was beautiful" said Miriam. "He was an old man with snow white hair. His costume was green coloured, with gold thread running through it; it was beautiful. He wore a ruff around his neck and if I had been a member of the public I would have thought that he was a role player in Elizabethan costume."
"In my own mind I wanted to go to find someone to come and see the ghost as well but I resisted leaving the room in case he had gone by the time I got back. Besides, I wanted to know where he would go to and how he would go. So I just stood in the doorway and watched him. I didn't take my eyes off him. I wanted him to turn around but he didn't." [50]

WRITER'S NOTE:

The fact that on this occasion Miriam stood her ground, so to speak, might have been due to her having had the earlier experience of a ghostly sighting. Perhaps this time she was mentally prepared and had more time to collect her thoughts. This contrasted with her earlier experience when the ghost was suddenly standing next to her. The writer continued the interview by asking some further questions:

[Question] Did you feel threatened in any way?

[Answer] "No not at all. I just stood there and watched him. Then all of a sudden, it was just like pieces of dust; just like pieces of dust, going. I went over to the window to see if there were any pieces of dust on the floor but there was nothing".

[Question] Have you experienced anything else that was unusual during your time at the Tower?

[Answer] "There was a time when I was coming out of the Tapestry Bedroom when I thought I saw a moving figure from the corner of my eye. There was nothing there but afterwards I could smell the faint odour of perfume. There was yet another time when a man took lots of photographs; both inside and outside of the Tower. He took some of the main entrance door to the Tower and then he came into the reception to show me. On the photos of the door were orbs and inside the orbs there were faces, you could see them!"

MIRIAM'S FRIEND FEELS COLD

Before closing the chapter on Miriam's Tower experiences, the writer thinks that it is only fair to mention her friend Veronica. Miriam and Veronica both worked at the Tower during the second half of 1990. It would seem that the large wooden staircase, near the Tower entrance, has an affect on certain people. The reader will remember that earlier in this narrative, the writer described his introductory visit to the Tower and stated that as he crossed the staircase he 'felt' a 'presence' outside the Drawing Room.

In Veronica's case she remembers that when she first went to the Tower to be interviewed for her job, she was one of about fifteen people who were conducted around the buildings. When they arrived at the staircase and were standing outside the Chapel entrance, Veronica said she suddenly felt "cold" and "uneasy" but decided not to mention it. She also adds that during the whole of the time that she subsequently worked at the Tower, there was nothing further to report.

JOHN GARDINER

John Gardiner was born in the Lancashire town of Darwen, where he has lived for most of his life. He started working at Turton Tower during the 1990s in a part-time capacity and throughout the years has gained an extensive knowledge of the Tower's history. From the year 2008 until he retired in 2014 he was employed as the Heritage Building Supervisor and Tour Guide. The writer has spoken to John at length and has learnt about his paranormal encounters at the Tower. The following pages are a honest account of an interview that the writer conducted in June of 2013.

THE BRADSHAW BEDROOM APPARITION

At the start of the interview the writer followed John as he entered the Bradshaw Bedroom. He described it as a Victorian lady's guest bedroom having an adjoining dressing room. It was there that he told the writer about some of his paranormal experiences. When Bradshaw Hall was demolished, two of its fireplaces were taken and re-assembled at Turton Tower. One was installed in the room that serves as the visitors reception area and the other was placed in the Bradshaw Bedroom. The bedroom also gained a four-poster bed that originated from Bradshaw Hall. On either side of the bed is a doorway, with the one nearest to the fireplace opening into the adjoining dressing room. Similarly, the bedroom's main entrance door is situated next to the other side of the bed.

John claims that when entering the dressing room from the bedroom, he feels very uneasy. He said, "The adjoining door does make me feel funny, it makes the hairs stand up on my arms and the back of my neck and I try to avoid walking through that doorway. Conversely, if I enter the dressing-room from its main entrance door I'm all right; it's just that particular doorway that I don't like."

The dressing room has two doors, one that connects with the Bradshaw Bedroom and the other that allows access from the stairs landing area. It may be noted that the main entrance door to the Bradshaw Bedroom and the dressing room's main entrance door, share access from a common stairs landing area. As John and the writer stood next to the four-poster bed John began to recount his paranormal encounters.

"This room in particular does bring back some uneasy feelings for me. It was the year 2011, early in the season, about May or June, when I was locking up one evening and in a bit of a rush to get home. What I would normally have done was to come in, (from the stairs landing area) close the blinds, pull the curtains, turn the light out and lock the door behind me. I would then go into the dressing room (from the stairs landing area) and do the same. Being a creature of habit this is what I would normally do but on this particular day I decided that I would save a couple of minutes.

This time after entering the bedroom (from the landing area) I locked the door from the inside, turned the light out, pulled the blinds and closed the curtains. I then walked towards the adjoining door with the intention of entering the dressing room. As I got to the corner of the bed, nearest to the fireplace, I suddenly felt that I was not on my own. As I turned around thinking that I might have locked a visitor in, I noted there was nobody there. What happened next and the only way I can explain it; is when you get a strong ray of sunlight shining through a window and you see the little sparkly bits of dust.

The entire room exploded into all these tiny sparkly bits of dust but there was no light coming in, because the blinds were closed. The light was out, the curtains were closed and it was virtually total darkness. And I got out very quickly!"

Photo No 34 (circa: 2014)
The Bradshaw Bedroom

Pictured in Photo No 34 are the four-poster bed and the stone fire-place that originally came from Bradshaw Hall, at the time when it was demolished. Two doorways can be seen that are mentioned in the text. The one on the left of the bed leads into the en-suite dressing room whilst the one on the right is the main entrance door leading from the stairs landing area.

UNSEEN CONTACT IN THE BRADSHAW BEDROOM

No sooner had the writer absorbed what John had shared regarding the 'sparkly bits of dust', when he began to relate a second occurrence:

> "Another experience I have had in this room
> was in September of the year 2012, when I

brought a party of people around for a guided tour. I always stand next to the corner of the four-poster bed nearest to the main entrance door whilst the visitors gather around the fireplace area. A lady, who was stood in front of and nearest to the fireplace, suddenly accused me of touching her face. Then all of a sudden, she fell backwards and accused me of pushing her over. She fell backwards knocking over the fire-screen, the bed-pan and the bed warmers, which were sent flying. Then she accused me of pushing her."

John explained that from where he was standing in relation to the lady, it was not possible for his hand to reach her face. Indeed, the distance from the corner of the bed where John was standing, to the fireplace where the lady was standing, was over six feet in distance. Of course it must be remembered that the other members of the group that were present, of which John states were about "five or six," would have witnessed anything untoward that may have taken place.

MOVING FURNITURE IN THE BRADSHAW ROOM

One Monday morning, during November of 2013, John arrived at the Tower to begin his routine chores. The night before, following his usual inspection of the premises, he had locked all the doors and gone home. At this time of the year the Tower is generally closed to the public and re-opens for the new season beginning in March. However, a guided tour can sometimes be arranged during this period, if for example, a party of school children might wish to visit. John makes daily trips to the Tower to make sure that the central heating system is functioning and that generally all is in order within the building. The Tower is protected from unwanted intruders by an alarm system, that is activated by passive infrared detectors.

John asserts that after he had locked-up the night before, no one could have gained access to the Tower without his knowledge and certainly not before his arrival on the Monday morning. It turned out that when he unlocked the door of the Bradshaw Bedroom, there was a surprise waiting for him.

As John began to describe the unexpected experience, he took hold of a stand chair. It is kept at the side of the four-poster bed and nearest to the dressing room door. He then placed it in front of the fireplace and against the hearth. The distance being about a metre from the bed. He proceeded to describe what he had seen.

> "When I came into the room on the Monday morning, this chair had moved from being next to the bed and was placed next to the fireplace. All the carpet was wrinkled up underneath the chair; as though the chair had been pushed backwards along the floor and away from the hearth and had caused the carpet to crumple up. Also the top edges of the bed clothes, on both sides of the bed, were turned back at the corners; just as if someone had just got out of bed!"

WRITER'S NOTE:

It may be seen from Photo No 34, that the chair John mentions is placed to the left of the bed and next to the dressing room doorway. The fireplace near the left front corner of the bed is where the visitors were standing when the lady was 'pushed' by the invisible force.

THE GHOSTLY HAND PUSHING A DOOR

John Gardiner had no further stories to tell about the Bradshaw Bedroom. However, he did recall an occasion when he was on duty at the main reception desk of the Tower. Sometimes it is necessary for John to work at the reception desk where visitors would pay their entrance fee.

From there they would be directed around the museum. It was on one such occasion that a man asked if he could take photographs both inside and outside the building. John takes up the story:

> "One other strange occurrence that has happened about eighteen months to two years ago, (about mid 2012) was when I had to work on reception, which I don't particularly like doing. A gentleman arrived as a visitor and signed a disclaimer to say that he could take photographs without using a flash gun. After he had been around the house taking photographs he went outside and proceeded to take photographs of the outside of the buildings, which included one or two of the large wooden front doors. (The doors open into the reception area of the original peel Tower.)
>
> He was using a digital camera and after taking a picture of the front door, he was amazed to see an unusual image on the camera's viewing screen. He came running into the reception and showed me the camera's pictures. The unusual image showed the large front door, having a 'big orange circle' in front of it and with a 'hand' inside the circle, which appeared to be pushing against the door. He said he was going to e-mail me a copy of it but I haven't received an e-mail as yet."

THE VICTORIAN TEA ROOM'S GHOSTLY DOG

During my interview with John I asked him if he had heard of any dog sightings.

> "Oh yes," he said "My daughter has seen a dog! (John's daughter is an adult) It was about eighteen months ago (January 2012) and it was my weekend off duty from work. On the Sunday morning we were having a drink of tea in the Tower's Victorian tea room. The tea room was reasonably full and all of a

sudden my daughter jumped up from her chair and exclaimed, "Go on, get out, get out!" as she waved her arms in an ushering gesture. "You can't come in here; this is a tea room; go on get out!" she said. Everyone looked at her as though she had gone crackers. She turned to me and said more quietly, "Did nobody else see that dog?"

Later that morning we went into the Tower and into the Ashworth Room where there is a photograph album. As my daughter was paging through the book she suddenly said, "There; that's the dog!" and she pointed to a photograph of a small dog. It looked like a border collie and was pictured seated next to a 19th century local man who was named John Wood."

WRITER'S NOTE:

It is not known if the dog lived or indeed died at the Tower. The important point to note is that the dog 'seen' by John's daughter, was the same breed as the one in the photograph. Furthermore, she made the comparison whilst her memory of the sighting was still fresh.

THE CHAPEL ROOM

'The Chapel' is the name given to a room on the first floor of the Tower. It is accessed from the main staircase. Attached to it is a smaller room known as the 'Priest's Room'. At times during the life of the Tower a travelling Catholic priest might visit. The rooms would be used by the priest to conduct mass. The attendees being members of the household and possibly invited guests. There have been some notable paranormal happenings both inside the Chapel and its immediate vicinity.

THE MAN WITH THE BAD TEETH

Whilst John and I were standing in the Chapel Room, he told me the story about a family who he guessed were of African origin. He had shown them around the Tower in the year 2000. They had got as far as the Chapel Room and as John recalled; "The little boy, who at that time was four and a half years of age, entered the Chapel Room. He suddenly ran out very quickly and proceeded down the stairs before running out of the Tower screaming!" John explained that the little boy had claimed to have 'seen' a man standing in the Chapel Room. He was wearing dark clothes and having black hair, a big black beard and bad teeth. It transpired that six months later, the little boy was still having nightmares about the man!

The boy's parents were quite concerned for the child's welfare. They decided to take him back to the Tower. Their intention was to prove that there was nothing in the Chapel Room that could cause him any harm. The parents of course had seen nothing untoward at the time of the incident. When they arrived at the Chapel entrance the little boy refused to go into the room. Although this time he didn't run off screaming. John explained that the family departed from the Tower but returned yet again in the early part of 2013. On this occasion the young boy actually entered the Chapel but didn't stay long. He was heard to say to his parents, "That man is still here!"

John noticed that the little boy's younger brother, who was with him on this occasion, looked a "little bit upset". Perhaps significantly, it was noted that the younger brother was now the same age that the little boy had been, at the time they had first visited the Tower. John recalled that the boys only entered the Chapel to satisfy their curiosity. Then they left the Tower very quickly. He surmised that it was hardly likely that the little boy of such a tender age, could maintain the same story for a period lasting over six months. Unless, as John remarked, he was "A very clever little boy."

THE LADY AND THE PERFUME

A final story that John offered the writer was that of a ghostly woman, who was said to have been seen by some employees of a security company.

About the year 2010, security guards made regular nightly calls to the Tower. They made sure that all the doors and gates were secure. On one occasion as they approached the upper car park, near to the Victorian Tea Room, the headlights of their vehicle picked out the ghostly form of a young woman.

The woman was seen close to the ruins of a small building, which stands on the north-east corner of the vegetable garden. The guards didn't expect to see anyone at that time of the evening. But in keeping with their responsibilities, they decided to go over to the woman and to inquire as to why she was there. They left their vehicle on the car park with its headlights switched on, so as to provide maximum light. They walked towards the derelict building, using the light from their torches to illuminate their way. As they approached to within a few feet of the lady, she suddenly disappeared!

Naturally taken aback, the two guards were somewhat confused. None the less they completed their walk up to the spot where the lady had been. They looked around the immediate area for any sign of her whereabouts but she was not to be found. However, there was one thing that they both noticed and both agreed upon. It was the odour of the lady's perfume that hung in the air!

THE LIGHT IN THE WINDOW

Tony Lee, is a qualified electrician and lives at Bradshaw, near Bolton. For a hobby he enjoys taking part in military re-enactments. Periodically he dons an American army uniform and joins a group of enthusiasts. They meet with their pseudo German adversaries to engage in mock battles.

On a warm and dry evening of May 31st 2013, the front lawn of Turton Tower was transformed into a WW2 American-styled military camp. Most of the tents were pitched on the lawn area to the front of the peel Tower. Tony had his tent pitched separately. It was located on the grass verge and nearest to the wooden gates at the main entrance. He hastened to point out that at night time the area surrounding the Tower is "very dark!" Sometime during the evening Tony's immediate group of friends decided to 'whet their whistle' and head on down to a local public house.

Photo No 35 (circa: 2014)
Tony Lee and his WW2 Jeep

They travelled of course in style aboard their vintage American Jeep. The other members of the group, who were playing the role of German soldiers, chose to remain behind. As Tony said, "Since they were young lads and not having a lot of money to warrant a visit to the pub they stayed at the camp to keep an eye or two on things." When Tony and his friends returned to the camp a couple of hours later, they were met by a few of the camp guardians who posed a pertinent question. "Is, the Manager still inside the Tower?" Tony thought for a second or so and answered, "No; the place is locked up for the night and all the staff have gone home."

The guardians' spokesperson explained that after Tony and his friends had vacated the camp, which was around nine o' clock that night, their group had seen a light shining from one of the Tower's rooms. But more importantly it was 'going on and then off.' When Tony asked where exactly this was taking place, the spokesperson pointed to a room that was just above the side entrance door. In fact the room serves as the office to the Tower Manager and is immediately above the public entrance area and the souvenir shop. The incident had occurred enough times to command the attention of a few people and all of them had seen the light 'going on and then off.'

WRITER'S NOTE:

The writer looked at the room in question and took particular notice of the light fitting that is installed there. It is a simple twin-tube fluorescent unit having a diffuser fitted to it and it is operated by a standard one-way wall switch. After questioning a member of the staff it was understood that no incidents of any kind concerning the light, had ever been reported in the past. Furthermore, the writer established that there was an intruder sensor fitted inside the office room. It was of the passive infrared type and could not emit any light that would be enough to illuminate the room. It would of course trigger the alarm system if anyone should enter. Tony Lee knows a thing or two about electricity and it was from him that a possible explanation was given.

Tony said, "A fluorescent tube can sometimes glow without being switched on." He recalled that once during his career he was called to a job where a fluorescent light was said to be 'still switched on' although the operating switch was in the 'off' position. He said that as he looked up at the light fitting, he could see what appeared to be like 'smoke rings' inside the fluorescent tube. They gave the impression that they were moving along the length of the tube from one end to the other.

This action caused the tube to emit light, albeit not half as strong as if it operated normally. Tony investigated the phenomenon and eventually discovered that instead of the regulatory 'live' wire being switched, it was in fact the 'neutral' wire that was switched. This incorrect situation meant that there was a 'live' supply to the unit at all times, even though the light switch was in the 'off' position. The bogus 'live' supply was enough to partially activate the workings of the fitting and thus cause the tube to 'glow' and in the words of Tony Lee, "It was half igniting."

Tony also pointed out that under this condition the tubes experience a reduction in working life, which make it necessary to replace them more frequently. The writer looked into the possibility of Tony's explanation and found that the wiring to the Tower's office was in fact correct. Had it been otherwise, there would not have been enough light emitted to fully illuminate the office room. Additionally, the light would not be sufficient to arouse the attention of the military enthusiasts.

One must remember that the light was said to be 'going on and off' and under the condition suggested by Tony that would not have occurred. Another final point is that the fluorescent tube in the office light fitting, has lasted for a number of years and at the time of writing is still going strong.

The writer wonders if this incident could be the work of a poltergeist?

LITTLE RED RIDING HOOD

Of the many framed oil paintings that adorn the walls of Turton Tower, one painting in particular sprang to prominence in December of 2013. It was then that it mysteriously 'fell' from a wall. To the casual observer the incident would appear to have been the result of a faulty wall fixing. However, let the reader study the facts of the incident in greater detail.

The painting depicts a young girl who happens to be wearing a red hooded-cape. She appears to be walking in a wooded area. It naturally follows that because of this arrangement the painting is known as 'Little Red Riding Hood.' But it must be said that the canvas is unsigned and untitled. Furthermore, there is no image of any wolf present. Together with its gilded frame the painting measures 79 X 90 cm. Considering the style of the image it has been suggested that the artist may be Thomas Houston, of Bolton.

Photo No 36 (circa: 2014)
John Gardiner points to the wall where the painting
of Red Riding Hood was displayed:

112

The framed painting was hanging on a wall of the first floor that is situated opposite the entrance to the Chapel. A singular wire was strung across the back of the frame. The wire was hung onto two picture hooks that were fixed to the wall. Worm-screw shafts formed part of the picture hooks being just over an inch in total length. They were screwed into plastic wall plugs that had been inserted into the wall plaster. The writer saw that one of the picture hooks was still screwed into its plastic wall plug but had become detached from the wall in its entirety.

The incident occurred at a time when the building was empty of visitors. Mr Gardiner, who was the Building Supervisor and Mr Ian Moss, who was the Volunteers Supervisor, were on duty in the Tower. They were stood near the visitors' entrance area, which is located at the opposite end of the building to where the painting was displayed. They were engaged in conversation, when without any prior warning, they both heard the sound of a loud crash and thereafter went to investigate. When they arrived at the scene of the incident they found that the painting had apparently fallen from the wall and had dropped down on to the staircase. It appeared to have continued its journey down a few steps, before coming to a halt at a lower-level.

Although the oil painting was creased in a number of places, it was not extensively damaged. I believe it was due to the frame having taken the brunt of the impact. The canvas of the painting had pulled away from the frame on one length of the picture and the gilded frame was fractured. John Gardiner remarked, somewhat wryly, "What a shame, it was the only painting in the whole building in which the subject is smiling!" The painting may be viewed on-line at 'Art U.K. artworks' by copying and pasting the following url into the google search bar:
https://artuk.org/discover/artworks/little-red-riding-hood-152710/search/venue:turton-tower-6221/page/3#image-use

John Gardiner's remark about the girl in the painting is not strictly true. The writer looked at the painting more closely and was surprised to see that the girl is not smiling. She initially appears to be sticking her tongue out! However, in reality both assumptions are wrong. The girl just happens to have unusually large lips and depending on how the observer looks at the painting, determines the condition perceived.

It may be said that the framed painting fell from the wall because of its weight. Furthermore the screws and plastic wall plugs were of insufficient length to make an effective fixing to the wall.
Collectively, the weight of the frame, together with that of the canvas painting, was enough to pull the fixings out of the wall. Granted the wall plugs were short in length but it must be stated that the painting had hung from the wall by the method described, for many years. This fact is verified by Mr Gardiner who was employed at the Tower during that time.

Why then after so many years would the painting choose to fall down? The writer feels an alternative explanation would be to suggest poltergeist activity.

GHOST HUNTERS

Since the year 2014 organised groups of people calling themselves 'Ghost Hunters,' have conducted investigations at Turton Tower, in the hope of experiencing some paranormal encounter. 'Sixth-Sense Ghost Hunters' and 'Simply Paranormal' are two such groups who frequently conduct 'Ghost Hunts.' Their investigations are open to the fee-paying public and in February of 2015, the writer chose to purchase a ticket.

I attended an event held by the 'Sixth-Sense Ghost Hunters' and joined twenty-seven other members of the public who were split into smaller groups and with each group having a supervisor. The prime objective of the investigation was to put into action, a number of oui/ja boards, which were issued to the various groups. The intention was to use the oui/ja boards as a means by which to contact any spirit(s) that might be present at the Tower. The boards were printed with the normal letters of the alphabet as well as numbers from zero to nine and along with the complete words, 'Yes', 'No,' 'Hello,' and 'Bye Bye.' All the lettering was printed using luminous ink and was easily visible when the light of the chosen room was switched off.

For the benefit of the reader who is not familiar with the use of such boards the following explanation may be beneficial. A glass tumbler is placed upside down in the centre of the oui/ja board, which in itself measures approximately two feet square. The members of the group, who are seated in a circle surrounding the board, are each required to place just a finger tip on top of the glass. The finger tip must rest on top of the glass tumbler in an up-turned manner, so that no one can be suspected of pushing it. Questions are then asked by the supervisor, or a chosen spectator, of any spirit(s) that may be present within the room. The spirit is expected to answer the enquirer by spelling out a word(s) on the board by pushing the glass towards each letter of a word in turn.

Mr Ian Wood was the organiser of the ghost-hunt and it was he who gave the assembly a prep-talk, before it was divided into various small groups. Each group was then taken to an allocated room from where the investigations began.

Photo No 37 (circa: 2015)
Mr Ian Wood (centre) with his team of 'Ghost Hunters' operating a oui/ja board:

Mr Wood explained that a previous visit to the Tower had produced an unusual, if not impossible result. After the light was switched off in the room that was under investigation, a strange thing occurred. The oui/ja board that was about to be used suddenly became darkened. All the letters, numbers and words could not be seen; except for the singular word, 'Hello.'

During the evening of the 'Ghost Hunt' in which the writer was present, a couple of notable happenings took place. Whilst seated in the Tapestry Room, with a group of people who were using an oui/ja board, suddenly a radio receiver that was carried by our supervisor, burst into life. A voice from the radio enquired if anyone had vacated the room at anytime within the past few minutes. The reply of course was that everyone was seated and no one had moved out of the room. A conversation was then heard over the radio which was in contact with the supervisors of the other groups and also the Tower Manager, who generally remained in his office.

It was confirmed that everyone present that night and at the time in question had not left their respective rooms. However, one male member of a group, that had been sitting in the Ashworth Bedroom and which happened to have its door open, thought differently. The gentleman of the group said he happened to look through the bedroom doorway and saw movement on the staircase, which was at the end of a connecting passage outside the bedroom. What he saw was a dark figure that appeared to walk through a wall, which happened to be an outer wall of the Tower.

A second happening occurred sometime later, when another group who were operating their oui/ja board, received a message. The gist of the message was that it came from a young girl of 14 years of age, who called herself 'Lizzie'. It would seem that according to her confession to the group, she had become pregnant at some time during her life and had given birth to an illegitimate child.

At the end of the 'Ghost Hunt,' which began at eight o'clock in the evening and lasted until two the following morning, Ian Wood conducted a simple ceremony that was designed to protect everyone upon leaving the Tower. He wanted to be sure that every visitor leaving the Tower did so without any ghostly adherent.

In reference to the occurrence of paranormal happenings, Mr Wood closed the event by making a statement about the possibility of the existence of ghosts. He said, "With all respect to everyone; but we're all ignorant if we say that there's nothing out there."

CONCLUSION

This narrative attempts to compile the many mysterious tales having some connection with Turton Tower. They begin in the early part of Queen Victoria's reign and span a period of more than a hundred years. Some of the stories can be explained rationally. There's the one about the rodent who managed to roll potatoes down the Tower's main staircase. The action gave rise to the notion that a 'boggart' was in residence.

Then there were the very convincing photographs of the 'Spectre of the Tower' but which raised debateable questions as to their authenticity. There were also stories of a personal nature, like the ones told by Miriam Disley. She had visual encounters with 'ghosts.' There is also the sighting made by the security guards. They saw a ghostly woman near the vegetable garden. As they approached her she disappeared leaving behind nothing but the odour of her perfume in the air. How can one argue with actual witnesses to such sightings?

Other stories to consider are those relating to Bradshaw Hall and Timberbottom Farm. Could it be that whatever was appearing at Bradshaw Hall has attached its energy to the relics from there? Similarly, could whatever that gave rise to the disturbances at Timberbottom Farm have followed the two skulls and taken up residence at Turton Tower? The 'hooded' figure that Miriam Disley encountered in the Bradshaw Room, may possibly be the 'monk' that was resident at Bradshaw Hall. After all, the fireplace and the furniture were all originally housed in the ancient building.

Finally, in the end it is you, the reader, who must look at the evidence put before you and decide. Do you believe that paranormal activities have taken place at Turton Tower or that they have not? But before reaching a decision, it might be prudent to consider the words of Mr. Ian Wood, the professional ghost hunter. It was he who said, "With all respect to everyone; but we're all ignorant if we say that there's nothing out there."

REFERENCES

[1]Harland, John, and Wilkinson, T. T., *Lancashire Legends Traditions, Pageants, Sports,* (London: George Routledge and sons, 1873), p.59.

[2] Jung, Carl & Pauli, W., *The Interpretation of Nature and the Psyche,* (London, 1955).

[3]Deschamps, Emile, Oeuvres Completes, Tomes I - VI, Reimpr. De l'ed. De Paris, 1872-74.

[4]Fodor, Nandor, *Encyclopaedia of Psychic Science,* (London: Arthurs Press, 1933).

[5]Grimshaw, Thomas, *General Course of the History, Science, Philosophy and Religion of Spiritualism,* (1973).

[6]The Harmonical Philosophy, (1917).

[7]Grimshaw, Thomas, *General Course of the History, Science, Philosophy and Religion of Spiritualism,* (1973).

[8]Barbanell, Maurice, *This Is Spiritualism,* (Oxshott: The Spiritual Truth Press, 1959).

[9]Harland, J, and Wilkinson, T. T., *Lancashire Legends,* 1873, p.60.

[10]Greenhalgh, J. D., *Notes on the History of the Township of Breightmet,* (Bolton: Tillotson & Son, 1879), p.23.

[11]Greenhalgh, *Notes on the History,* p.23.

[12]Greenhalgh, *Notes on the History,* p.23.

[13]Byan, Haggas, A., *Bradshaw Works Its History and Associations,* 1950, Bolton Library archives Ref: ZZ/606/1

[14]Albert Winstanley, *Traditions of Lancashire,* (1991).

[15] Ellis-Rae, Vivienne, *True Ghost Stories of our own time,* (Faber and Faber, London, 1990). p.157

[16]Price, Harry, *Poltergeist, Tales of the Supernatural,* (London: Bracken Books, 1993), p.p. 345-346.

[17]Price, *Poltergeist, Tales of,* p.p.345-346.

[18]Bolton Evening News, *'Ghostly Visits,'* Dec 21 1928, p.5.

[19]Bolton Journal and Guardian, *Ghost walks again,* October 27 1939.

[20]Bolton Journal and Guardian, *Ghost walks again,* October 27 1939.

[21]Bolton Evening News, *Ghosts won't go away,* September 25 1995, p.11.

[22]According to the Bolton Journal and Guardian of March 13 1953, p.7, Col. Hardcastle took the small skull to Manchester for repair on 7 December 1927.

[23]Bolton Evening News, *Ghosts won't go away,* September 25 1995, p.11.

[24]Bolton Evening News, *Skull-duggery afoot,* September 22 1995.

[25]Bolton Evening News, *'Mother Went Grey Overnight,'* September 29 1995, p.55.

[26]Bolton Evening News, September 21 1995.

[27]Bolton Evening News, September 21 1995.

[28]Ashworth, G. H., *Turton Tower Museum,* (Tillotsons Ltd., Bolton, 1945). Pp.19-25

[29]Byan, Haggas, A., *Bradshaw Works Its History and Associations,* 1950, Bolton Library archives Ref: ZZ/606/1

[30]Ashworth, G. H., *Turton Tower Museum,* (Tillotsons Ltd., Bolton, 1945). Pp.19-25

[31] Ellis-Rae, Vivienne, *True Ghost Stories of our own time,* (Faber and Faber, London, 1990). pp. 156-57.

[32]Bolton Evening News, 15 August 1989, p.3.

[33]Bolton Evening News, 15 August 1989, p.3.

[34]Bolton Evening News, *'Ghosts won't go away,'* September 25 1995, p.11.

[35]Bolton Evening News, *'Historic Bolton Landmark,'* June 7 1990, p.11.

[36]Bolton Journal and Guardian, December 23 1927.

[37] Bolton Journal and Guardian, December 23 1927.

[38]Shearer, Ellen, Victorian Children at Turton Tower, (Beric Tempest & Co. Ltd., St. Ives, Cornwall, 1982) p.16.

[39]A wide footpath runs parallel with the railway line at the rear of Turton Tower. Adjacent to the footpath is a stone built storage shed. Opposite this are a number of flat stones that are the remains of the 'monument' to which Doreen refers.

[40] *Scaffolding on fire,* Bolton Evening News, January 1955.

[41] *Scaffolding on fire,* Bolton Evening News, January 1955.

[42] *Bus driver saw a ghost near Turton Tower,* Bolton Evening News, April 14th 1954.

[43]*Bus driver saw a ghost near Turton Tower,* Bolton Evening News, April 14th 1954.

[44]http://www.bing.com/search?q=ghosts+of+north+west&form - Mystical World Wide Web-Ghosts of North West [Accessed 28/02/2015]

[45]Mr & Mrs Sam Weatherall, Bolton Evening News, 14th June, 1966.

[46]Tragically on the morning of November 17th 1967, Sam and Jean Weatherall heard the news that their daughter Moira and her friend Wendy Robson had died in a road accident. [Bolton Journal and Guardian, Friday November 17 1967, p.5.]

[47]Albert and Doris Walker, *Spirits in The Tower,* The Bolton Journal and Guardian, December 5th 1975, p.86.

[48]Albert and Doris Walker, *Spirits in the Tower,* The Bolton Journal and Guardian, December 5th 1975, p 86.

[49]*The Man Wearing a Top Hat*
Interview with Ken Holden (August 2014)

[50]Interview with Miriam Disley-December 2014

PHOTOGRAPH CREDITS

Photo No 1-Timberbottom Farm-[Bolton Evening News, 5/10/1995, p.86.]

Photo No 2-Timberbottom Farm-[Bolton Library Archives]

Photo No 3-Map of historical locations-[By permission of openstreetmap.org [Licensed CCBY-SA]

Photo No 4 & 5-Timberbottom Farm Lintel [Author's collection]

Photo No 6 & 7-Timberbottom Farm Skulls-[Author's collection]

Photo No 8-Bradshaw Brook-[Author's collection]

Photo No 9-Bradshaw Hall-[Bolton Library Archives]

Photo No 10-Bradshaw Works-oil painting by G S Fletcher 1951-Printed Bolton Evening News 15/12/2003. p.21. [Bolton Library Archives]

Photo No 11-Col. H. M. Hardcastle-[Bolton Library Archives]

Photo No 12-Ruins Bradshaw Hall Porch-By courtesy of RNN Ltd Newspaper, Bolton, 23/08/1989.[Bolton Library Archives]

Photo No 13-Bradshaw Hall Porch-Author's collection

Photo No 14-Turton Tower-[Author's collection]

Photo No 15- Col. Sir Lees Knowles by courtesy of Fusilier Museum, Bury, U.K.

Photo No 16-Alderman G. H. Ashworth-[Author's collection] by courtesy of Turton Tower.

Photo No 17-Floor Plan-[Adapted from: The Victoria History of the County of Lancaster-Farrer & Brownbill, Vol 5, p.277]

Photo No 18-Doreen Hough-[Author's collection]

Photo No 19-Turton Tower sitting room-[Author's collection] by courtesy of Doreen Hough

Photo No 20-Fire at Turton Tower-[Bolton Evening News-January 1955]

Photo No 21-Albert Barrett-[Author's collection] by courtesy of Doreen Hough

Photo No 22-Turton Tower's bus stop. [Author's collection]

Photo No 23-Sam Weatherall-[Bolton Evening News-June 1966]

Photo No 24-Rocking cradle-[Author's collection]

Photo No 25 and Photo No 26-Entrance area Turton Tower-[Barbara Fisher collection]

Photo No 27&28-Ghostly form-[Barbara Fisher collection]

Photos No 29-30-31-31A-31B-32&33-Lizzie Jones-[Author's collection]

Photo No 34-Bradshaw Bedroom-[Author's collection]

Photo No 35-Tony Lee-[Author's collection]

Photo No 36-John Gardiner-[Author's collection]
Photo No 37-'Sixth Sense' Ghost Hunters-[Author's collection]
Book cover photos of Turton Tower [Author's collection]
Art work by Brian Mills at www.bmillsdesigns.co.uk

BIBLIOGRAPHY

Ashworth, G. H., *Turton Tower Museum,* (Tillotsons Ltd., Bolton, 1945).

Brownbill, J., & Farrer, W., *The History of the County of Lancaster,* (Dawsons of Pall Mall, London Vol.5., 1911)

Barbanell, Maurice, *This Is Spiritualism,* (The Spiritual Truth Press, Oxshott, 1959).

Ellis-Rae, Vivienne, *True Ghost Stories of our own time,* (Faber and Faber, London, 1990)

Fodor, Nandor, *Encyclopaedia of Psychic Science,* (Arthurs Press, London, 1933).

Greenhalgh, J. D., *Notes on the History of the Township of Breightmet,* (Tillotson & Son, Publishers, Bolton, 1879).

Harland, John, & Wilkinson, T. T., *Lancashire Legends Traditions, Pageants, Sports,* (George Routledge & Sons, London, 1873).

Jung, Carl & Pauli, W., *The Interpretation of Nature and the Psyche,* (London, 1955).

Price, Harry, *Poltergeist, Tales of the Supernatural,* (Bracken Books, London, 1993).

Shearer, Ellen, *Victorian Children at Turton Tower,* (Beric Tempest & Co. Ltd., St. Ives, Cornwall, 1982)

WEBSITE

http:/www.bing.com/search?q=ghosts+of+north+west&form
Mystical World Wide Web-Ghosts of North West [Accessed 28/02/2015]

Lightning Source UK Ltd.
Milton Keynes UK
UKHW02f1132290718
326375UK00005B/65/P